# TOO WEIRD FOR ZIGGY

Also by Sylvie Simmons:

*Serge Gainsbourg: A Fistful of Gitanes*

*Neil Young: Reflections in Broken Glass*

# TOO WEIRD FOR ZIGGY

## Sylvie Simmons

**Black Cat**
*New York*
a paperback original imprint of Grove/Atlantic, Inc.

*Published simultaneously in Canada*
*Printed in the United States ofAmerica*

FIRST EDITION

Library of Congress Cataloging-in-Publication Data

Simmons, Sylvie.
    Too weird for Ziggy / Sylvie Simmons.
    p. cm.
    ISBN 0-8021-4156-0
    1. Great Britain—Social life and customs—Fiction.   2. Rock musicians—Fiction.   3. Music trade—Fiction.   I. Title.

PR6119.I46L56 2004
823'.92—dc22                                                      2004052318

Black Cat
a paperback original imprint of Grove/Atlantic, Inc.
841 Broadway
New York, NY 10003

04 05 06 07 08   10 9 8 7 6 5 4 3 2 1

# CONTENTS

# PUSSY

I can't say I liked her, though I talked to her enough times, every time a new album or a tour came along. And then she disappeared, simply dematerialized. I don't think I'd thought about her until that night at the Conrad.

She had, like a lot of stars, a very big head. Not big as in arrogant, big as in oversized for her body like a doll, or like one of those space alien photos in the *National Enquirer*. A feline face, but like a child's drawing of a cat: big round head, big almond eyes, exaggerated cheekbones, and a pink marshmallow mouth neatly outlined and filled in like in a coloring book. And this tiny body. Like she'd had everything below the neck liposuctioned and injected into her lips.

Editors would send me along for the "female perspective," since the male journalists would simply worship and leave puddles on the floor. I'd do the hey, we're both girls, you can trust me trick, you know, bind us together with some sort of spiritual fallopian tube. But she'd look about her vaguely like a queen, or like a cow grazing, stare straight past me like her poster must have stared from the walls of teenage bedrooms up and down the country past all those hot-faced boys with their spongy Kleenexed palms. She'd recite her answers in a voice as dull and flat as Holland, and my mind would wander and I'd glance guiltily at the tape recorder to see if it had switched off too.

People called her Pussy and it pissed her off. She wasn't Pussy, she'd say, bored and sullen. Pussy was the

3

band. She was the singer. The voice of a child explaining something to its mother. They'd sent out promo baseball caps saying "Pussy Is a Group"—Terri Allen and four men. She lived with one of them, Taylor, the guitar player. He was small and dark with bright eyes black as T-shirts and a paddle nose like a little tit ironed on top. He looked like what you'd get if you let Roman Polanski and Michael Hutchence go to the Saturday night dance unchaperoned. His hands were tiny; he had to have his guitars custom-made to fit them. He'd sit in on the interviews off-piste, observing, saying nothing, merely exuding a practiced intensity, flopped like a noodle over the arm of a chair. He formed the band, he wrote the songs, he produced the records, and he fucked everything that didn't crawl away fast enough.

One time I watched him pick up the publicist— during the interview, right in front of both of us, while Pussy sat there like a still life, balancing that huge head on her neck by an enormous act of will. He gestured the woman out and down the hotel corridor. I heard another room door open and close. The publicist told me—a long time later, after he'd fired her for contradicting him and replaced her with some guy who used to run the fan club—that he didn't say anything, just pulled up her dress and put his hand up her. She said she felt like a ventriloquist's doll.

At the outset he'd make a point of speaking to the press before Pussy did, meeting the boys—it was usually boys—in the bar. He'd stroke their brains, flatter their intelligence, wrap the whole stupid-kewpie thing in a web of irony and convolution, letting them feel in on an intellectual joke. He'd remind them of the arty band he had before he found her working as a waitress in a cocktail bar. Then primed, male-bonded, male chauvinist Pygmalions, they'd be led in to talk to her. And she'd chafe at their assumption that she was his creation, that he was the screenwriter, the director, the whole fucking play, that she was just the bottle-blonde stuck up front to look pretty. Yet all the while she sat straight in her chair and mouthed his lines through her pink-pillow lips. And they'd nod sympathetically, leaning toward her, within lipstick-sniffing distance of the dreamy face, the disheveled, bleached hair, the colossal goddess head on the little girl's body, small and curved with a huge sphere on top, like that roll-on deodorant with the big wide ball.

Now that I think of it I do remember seeing something, in the whatever-happened-to section of a music magazine. The writer couldn't answer and threw the question open, and letters came in—one from the old drummer, self-publicizing a project he was doing with Philip Glass, and one from some New Yorker claiming he'd trailed her through Central Park. He said she looked like a bag lady, middle-aged and lumpy, and she was mumbling to herself the lyrics for a batch of new songs. He followed at a distance, he said, taking notes, and they printed this dreadful teenage poem about sex and murder that anyone could see the wacko had written himself.

Of course no one believed him, though I suppose it could have happened. You just wonder how someone, no matter how they've aged, even if their face and body have altered out of all recognition, how they can pass unnoticed among ordinary people when, at some point in their life, a hundred thousand boys have jerked off to their photograph or gazed up at them in the spotlight from down dark in the crowd. Something like that must be tattooed all over you. It must leave the kind of mark that can't be covered up.

There was a bunch of us at the Conrad in a corner of the lobby over by the window, the rain sheeting down outside. Interviews were running late as usual, and by early evening there were seven or eight of us backlogged, bitching, drinking, running up the record company's tab. We were killing time telling old war stories and swapping gossip— just enough to swell your reputation, not enough to give the competition something to print. I'm trying to remember how the conversation got around to Pussy. That's it, there was a slime from the tabloids sitting with us, telling sick jokes about Freddie Mercury and AIDS. When they finally scraped him off the seat and took him upstairs for his interview, we all started talking about rock stars who'd died, and Pussy's guitarist came up.

They shot Taylor's funeral for a video for the tribute album. Fat, nasty paparazzi jostled through the crosses and stone angels for the best hanky-clutching celebrity shots. The place was black with rockstars; at least most of them didn't have to buy special clothes. Quite a production it was too. The coffin was shaped like a guitar case, according to his instructions, although they left out the window he wanted on top—so he could lie there and watch the goings-on, I suppose, silently, like he always had done; but no one fancied looking at a hundred and twenty pounds of mincemeat. It was a car wreck; quick but messy. Record company people, promoters, musicians played their parts professionally. Two of his girlfriends looked videogenically stricken, various relatives looked lost and out of place. And the band, as they walked in, were self-consciously solemn. There would be a jam session later on.

The minister arrived. She walked beside him, a tiny figure in a short black dress and a black Jackie Kennedy hat with a veil that came down to just above her lips, which trembled as she stood by the hole in the ground scraping her thumbnail up and down the stem of the rose she held in her hand. Then everyone filed around the grave in choreo-graphed misery, a whir of camera motor drives started up a rhythm, the minister's dusty old voice came in on lead, and as the coffin was lowered into the ground the first fat rain-drop percussed onto the camcorder lens, blurring the pic-ture. And that was that. Afterward I forgot all about her. We all did. That's the thing with this business, someone else always comes along.

Though I do recall seeing a photo in the papers. It was when they released the greatest hits album—this was years ago, Pussy had stopped doing press, but a New York photog-rapher shot her walking down the street. She looked fuzzy and fragmented in the picture, grainy. Like those old newspaper photos of the Rolling Stones' ex-girlfriends when they'd moved on from methadone to menopause before fading right away. The photo seemed inverted. Her body was bloated and her face seemed smaller. She was biting her mouth; it looked as if she might have punctured her lips and the flesh had all run down her neck and settled down below.

So we're in the hotel lobby, empty bottles and glasses piling up on the low table, and the PR has come down to lead the next victim upstairs when this young guy who freelances for one of the rock weeklies says he's just done an interview with Pussy. I missed the start—I was watching another journalist announce his arrival at the reception desk, and anyway, it's a well-known journalistic trait, switching off when someone's soliloquizing, figuring you'll catch it when you play the tape back later on. It's a habit, like people who use the video remote to try and fast-forward when it's the television, not a video, that's on.

When I plugged back in, he was telling how, after Taylor's funeral, Pussy had gone back to New York and lived there for a while with her old wardrobe girl. Then she came back to England, had an affair with the band's manager, Jack Mackie, and moved in with him.

"He was talking about putting something together with her—he'd hooked up with some musicians and written some songs that he thought would work great with her voice. He was one of those managers—you come across them now and then—who really want to be in the band. But she left him," said the freelance. "And she left the music business. She said she wanted to be by herself for a while. That she was coming on for forty and it sounded ridiculous but she'd never in her life ever lived on her own. So she went back to New York, told Mackie she'd call him with her address and phone number, but she never did. She didn't contact anyone. She just fell off the map."

"Hold the front fucking page," sneered the guy from 'XO, looking up from the new mobile phone whose display he had been studying with fascination ever since he arrived.

"Fuck you," said the freelance, reddening. He slid his thin butt to the edge of his seat and leaned forward. The pair stared each other down for a few moments until each was satisfied he'd won. Cheeks still hot, the freelance reached for his beer, identifying it from the dozen identical bottles littering the coffee table with the acumen of a mother bird locating its eggs. He threw his head back theatrically and drained the bottle dry.

"For Christ's sake stop giving the bottle a blow job and get the fuck on with it," said the man from *N.M.E.*

"If you'd shut the fuck up and let me I will." He propped his boots on the edge of the coffee table and sank back in his chair.

"Of course, it's not that difficult disappearing in a huge metropolis like New York, but the music business is like a village. Everyone knows what everyone is doing before they've even e-mailed their lawyer about doing it. But Pussy's manager never could find her. And it wasn't for lack of trying. Jack Mackie spent a fortune taking out ads in all the major music magazines; women's magazines too. He hired a publicist to plant stories in the newspapers: that this film director she really liked wanted her to star in his next movie; that her old wardrobe girl was pregnant and planning to get married and wanted her to be bridesmaid; that her favorite bodyguard was dying of cancer and wanted to see her one last time before he rearranged his final face. Mackie said anything and everything, but nothing flushed her out.

"You've got to give the man credit for persistence. Finally—after years it must have been—he found out where she was. She was renting a tiny one-room apartment in a low-life neighborhood in New York. Of course, with her money she could have easily bought one in the best part of town if she'd wanted to, but then it would have been simpler to track her down. And she didn't want to be tracked down—she didn't even have a telephone. Once Mackie got the address, he bombarded her with telegrams she never replied to. So he got on a plane and flew over to New York.

"Her flat was in one of those grim detective-movie buildings—rubbish in the hallway, kids running about everywhere. She was on the second floor at the end of the corridor by the fire escape. He rang the bell. She didn't answer. But he could sense she was in there. He came back several times that day and tried again. The next day too. But she still didn't answer. By now Mackie was getting pretty pissed off. He was hammering on the door and shouting, made such a racket one of her neighbors came out and threatened to do him over. So the following day he hired a couple of heavies and went back with them. 'I've come five fucking thousand miles,' he said, 'and I'm not leaving until you open this door.' She didn't. So Mackie said, 'Break it down.' A swift boot to the lock and it caved right in. But as Mackie went to open the door, it barely moved. It had jammed against something solid."

He stopped. We were all watching him now.

"And . . . ?" said the barnacle-faced man from the *Times*. He had just seen the PR heading over to take him up for his interview and wanted to get the punch line before he left.

The freelance picked up his bottle and held it vertically over his lips, forgetting for the moment that it was empty. But he was undisconcerted—he had our attention now and he was basking in it like a turtle on a rock. He puffed out his hollow chest and stretched out his thin arms.

"You'll have to wait till the story's published."

"Wanker," the *Times* man growled, and swept out.

The freelance grinned at us conspiratorially. "I'm not going to give some prick from the nationals a free story, am I? So anyway. One of the gorillas puts his shoulder to the door and manages to shove whatever it is aside. Mackie, feeling uneasier than he could ever remember feeling in his life, peered around the door. It was a metal filing cabinet. The place was full of them. Cabinets and cartons and cardboard file drawers. Though they couldn't make them out at first—it was so dark in there—there was a huge commercial refrigerator in front of the window blocking out most of the light."

And then he saw her. She was pale as veal cattle; she'd been shut away for years. Her face was big and moon-white, her blonde hair now brown and smooth as a conker. Amid this city of cabinets, she looked contained and compact, everything held tightly in, like when you drive your car between a small gap in the traffic and hold your breath and pull yourself in at the edges to try and fit in the space. Next to her the hired men looked deformed, like giants. Mackie gestured to them to wait outside in the hallway. They stood there, still as mountains, while the manager opened, one after another, the cabinet drawers.

They were full of folders, every one of them neatly filed and tabulated. Each folder held a number of sandwich bags, zipped tight and tagged in the corner with a label, written out in her neat little handwriting. Some of them appeared to be empty, a flat transparent square with dust and condensation trapped inside. The manager held it up to the little patch of light above the refrigerator. It could have been dandruff or a scraping of cocaine.

In the next cabinet he opened there were even more sandwich bags. Mackie lifted up a file and took out a bag at random. This time he could see what was in there, but it didn't help, none of it made any sense. It was hair—a tangled clump like you pull out of the plughole in the bathtub. The other bags had hair in them too. Sometimes just a strand or two, sometimes a handful.

In the top drawer the hairs were pale blonde with a smudge of brown on the crumb-tip. By the bottom drawer they were all brown. There were separate bags for eyelashes, and others stuffed with crunchy pubic hairs, like small, black springs squashed flat. And all of them were labeled with date and location, whether they'd been tugged from a hairbrush, culled from the sink, or swept up off the floor. The room was filled from top to bottom with bits of her—bits shed and hoarded, grouped and subgrouped, collected, catalogued, and safely filed away. The floor, every surface in the place, was immaculate. The dust from her dead skin cells had been brushed up and bagged as soon as it fell. There were bags of fingernails, tiny white crescents, and of toenail clippings curled thick and gray like dead wood lice.

And she just stood there watching him, small and hard and self-contained, as he went through all the cabinets, one by one, putting all the bags carefully back where he found them. She didn't say a word; he didn't either. He could hear an argument going on in the apartment upstair—banging, a child crying. It was the only sound in this small, stagnant room except for the whirring of the giant refrigerator.

"Where the fuck is that waitress?" the freelance suddenly demanded. "All this talking is making me thirsty."

A slender man in a smart black suit slipped out from behind his desk and walked briskly over. "Please keep it down," he said, "or I'm afraid I'm going to have to ask you to wait elsewhere. I'll send someone over to take your order."

"The manager turned to go," the freelance said, more quietly. "However much he'd needed to see Pussy before, what he needed now was to get out. Get some air. His legs felt unsteady. This was something he didn't know how to manage. But then he noticed the fridge. She was standing with her back to it, like a guard on sentry duty. The thing was bigger than she was. He knew he'd have to look in it before he left. As he approached, Pussy slid to one side. He ignored her and went straight for the chrome handle. Grabbing them, he tugged open the double doors."

A light came on, shining through the frozen fog like it does on the stage, fuzzy at the edges but sharp enough to pick out the cold sweat on Mackie's face. The right side of the fridge was almost empty—a carton of milk, some Coke cans, something unidentifiable wrapped up in a take-away bag. The freezer side, though, was almost full—with what looked like ice creams, neat rows of red-tipped Raspberry Ripples, steaming cold. And more Ziploc bags, puffed solid with frozen juice. He glanced over at Pussy, who was leaning against the bathroom door, arms crossed, hips thrust forward, one leg crossed over the other, swaying on the spot like a little girl.

"Mackie reached into the icy air and pulled one of the drawers out into the light. It was stacked with all her old used tampons and frozen bags of piss."

A couple of the male journalists started to look queasy. "Jesus," said one, "what a fucking nut." He stood up. "I'm gonna take a slash. If the waitress comes, mine's a Newcastle Brown." He went to the bathroom.

Mackie pushed open the bathroom door.

It was tiny, barely bigger than a mouse-mat; you had to walk sideways to squeeze inside. There was a sink and a big old tub, white and gleaming but for the crap-brown rust stain running down from the tap, and over in the corner there was a toilet. It had a two-drawer filing cabinet on top of it. In front, in this minuscule space, she'd jammed a chemical toilet, one of those things you use in caravans that desiccate your shit. The drawers were full of bags of gray-brown powder. She'd hung on to everything. There was not one single bit of her that was going to get away."

And that's all I heard. I was called up to do my interview. I suppose he'll get around to writing it up one day. What happened to her? All I know is the manager took her back with him to England. I hear she's making a comeback.

# GREETINGS FROM FINSBURY PARK

A man in a baggy blue suit custom-made not to fit stands by the carousel watching a lone unclaimed suitcase circle slowly around and around and around. He is thirty-eight, maybe forty years old, boy-thin and beautiful. His jacket, which would be loose on Arnold Schwarzenegger, has been pulled off one slim shoulder by the weight of a travel bag. His eyes are large and blue like his suit. His hair, straw-colored, is hacked off in a battered-child haircut you know cost the earth. A large leather suitcase appears at the top of the slide and one of the ground staff hurries over, as fast as her airline bondage skirt and stilettos will allow, and drags it off the carousel, deposits it with a flushed smile at his bashed-up Reeboked feet. He thanks her distractedly, hoists the shoulder bag back into place, turns the suitcase on its side, and wheels it toward the green channel.

Heathrow Customs. Thin wooden partitions, generically drab like a VD clinic, jerry-built into an alley where grim-faced men in uniform loiter on either side. Their eyes bore into you like they know the secrets of your soul as you walk past, trying to look normal, looking straight ahead to the open door where people are waiting, waving. But Spike can't look normal. Spike is a Star. He's used to being looked at. He's used to running the gauntlet while people gawk and scrutinize. But now he feels uncomfortable, his body feels tight and prickly under his loose clothes as Her Majesty's representatives stare at him with the familiar Englishman's challenge in their eyes, the reminder to a returning Brit of his original, unforgivable sin of ever having dared to leave.

One of the men gives the other the nod and he strolls up casually with that policeman's roll, the arrogant humility, the questions that are orders: "Excuse me sir? Could I ask you to step over here with your bags? If you'd like to put them up here? Right, sir, if I could take a look at your passport?"

And of course they know who he is. Everyone knows who he is. The postman, the bank manager, the cleaning lady, everybody knows everything about him, from the size of his pool to the size of his plonker. His last girlfriend, sweet young thing, sold her story to the papers. Over last Sunday morning's eggs and bacon, fifteen million of his fellow former countrymen learned that he's "hung like a horse," "rogers like a rabbit," and, completing the *ménagerie à trois*, "when he pulls his pants down, people throw buns at it."

It makes him smile; he's almost aroused for a second himself until a shiver shrivels his balls. They're going to want to take him in the back room and get his pants off so they can tell their mates in the pub tonight that they've seen Spike's tackle and the papers were lying well-they-do-don't-they. He'd had the rubber glove and flashlight enema so many times his arse was getting stretch marks—but that was a long time ago, back in the days when rockstars were open season for customs men, and you'd pull down your trousers with a flourish, like Malcolm McDowell in *If . . .* , and you'd bend over with a smirk of a man who knows that however unpleasant it is to have your rear end rummaged by a stranger it's a far far better thing than having to do the rummaging. But times have changed. Rockstar butts are clean now. Colonically irrigated. He feigns an unruffled nonchalance, a sublimely bored look on his face.

"Could I ask you where you've traveled from today, sir? Los Angeles? What was the purpose of your visit?" all the while looking down, thumbing through the well-worn pages tattooed with stamps and visas, stopping at the U.S green card. "Oh, of course. You live there." Spike can sense the menace behind the politeness. Very English. Predatory, but apologetically so. "Don't blame you. They did a survey. Over half the people living in England said they'd rather be living somewhere else. *Anywhere* else. You're well out of it, mate." Closing the passport up, handing it back to him. "Thank you, Mr. Mattock. Now if you wouldn't mind unlocking your suitcase?" He smells of dispenser soap and stale polyester. Spike casually turns the combination lock, lifts the leather lid. Hands pink from frequent washing shuffle, lift, and rummage.

"Well, well." The customs man has fished out a large pack of condoms and is brandishing it to the discreet amusement of the first-class passengers walking past. "Playing it safe then, Buttock?" Spike isn't listening; he stands there still as a photograph, gazing at nothing. The customs man raises his voice. "Haven't changed then, Buttock. Every time we landed in the shit, you'd be the one in the rubber suit." *Buttock.* His old school nickname. A flock of startled birds take off from his stomach. He focuses in on the customs man with a jolt.

A small man, thin but flabby. Crumbly white-gray complexion like a piece of old unchewed gum you find in your coat pocket a year later. Sparse hair—field mouse–colored once maybe, now house mouse-gray. Gray and dry like an ash sculpture but for the red hands and the two dots of red high on the cheeks. An old teacher, a friend of his father's? "You don't know who I am, do you, Buttock?"

Spike turns his full clear gaze on him. "I'm sorry—"

"John Dawes. Finsbury Park Grammar School for Boys." An edge to his voice. "Remember?"

And he tries. He really does. The name ricochets around inside his head like a pinball, shoots down alleyways and bounces off walls before dropping through the reject gap in the middle. It's hard when your past is just a press file of airbrushed photographs and quotable memories of memories. Spike mentally scans his record company biography and recent interviews for help. Nothing.

"Knocker Dawes. You borrowed my guitar. You touched up my sister. *You fucked my fucking wife!*" A laugh. Impossible to tell if he's inflicting humiliation or receiving it.

And suddenly Spike remembers. And a cold wave of guilt washes over him—a generic, all-purpose guilt encompassing everything, from failing to recognize an old friend to failing to be with his mother when she died and the last thing she hears about him being an eighteen-year-old girl's description of his dick. But no, he's jet-lagged, disoriented. Yesterday he was in Los Angeles in a recording studio, today he's in England, tomorrow's the funeral. Of course! His old friend, Knocker! Weird that another slice of his past should resurface right at this time. He offers him a full, photogenic smile.

"Thought I might run into you one of these days. I had Michael Caine through here a couple of weeks back. You meet a lot of people in this business, all walks of life. They don't say much though. In and out like a whorehouse. You wouldn't believe some of the scum we get through here, Buttock." The customs man has pulled a puffy square from the condom packet and is circling the rubber rim through the wrapper distractedly with forefinger and thumb. "If I had a fiver for every fuckwit who walks through here with a bellyload of drug-filled Durex–not a pretty sight, I'll tell you, when they burst. We had a bloke in the other day, swallowed a six-pack of heroin—two trainees in the back room spooning castor oil down his throat, waiting for it to come out the other end."

People walk by, recognize Spike, point him out. It embarrasses him suddenly, like he was caught showing off in front of a friend. The customs man watches them, eyebrows raised.

"They all love you, don't they? They all want to touch you, prostrate themselves in front of you. Look at that woman. It's running down her legs, she wants you so much. You can tell the English from the Americans. That lot are English. They know exactly who you are but they just walk by, pretending not to look, making out they're not impressed. This one, she's American."

A large woman detaches herself from her companion and comes over lopsidedly, weighed down on one side by a huge bag she keeps hitching back up onto her shoulder. She hooks her arm in his, her mouth two inches from his face. She says: "I know you."

He can smell in-flight champagne, slept-in clothes, a cocktail of trapped gas, and all the duty-free perfumes she tried on eleven hours ago. Spike looks straight into her eyes, not saying a word.

The customs man summons up the power of the entire British Government. "Madam. If you have something to declare, declare it *somewhere else.*"

"No need to be rude." She huffs back over to where her friend is waiting. "It *was* him, you know."

Spike feels a sinus headache kicking in. He always got them, flying. There was a curtain separating him from them but their bodies still intruded—the dust from their dead skin that circulated in the canned air for hours. The laundry smell of economy-section chicken mixed with the cheap burnt coffee kept the passages unblocked until he disembarked but then a swelling behind his eyes would try to force its way out of his nose and ears like balloons.

The customs man is turning over a pile of neatly folded clothes. He peels off a silk shirt, floppy, soft as skin, while Spike stands, hands in pockets, watching.

"Nice shirt. Expensive. You get to know these things in my line of work. I can tell straight off if something's fake. I can tell a phony Lacoste alligator at fifty yards. They think they've got it but they always make these little mistakes. I can tell you what fucking *street* in Hong Kong they bought the fake Rolex on. I know when I'm dealing with a big man or not. This shirt cost serious money. 'The Real Thing'—how much did you make on that song? Half a million? A million? A mate of mine's brother works for a record company. He says popstars make a fucking fortune on royalties, and they're mean as hell, the lot of them. Only time they put their hands in their pockets is to scratch their bollocks." Spike tugs his hands out of his pocket automatically.

"My daughter—she picked up your first album at a boot fair the other day. *50p.* You had some good songs on that one, I'll admit that. A lot more cheerful than the stuff you're doing now. Getting a bit jazzy in your old age, aren't you? Going for the cred market? Can't whistle the new songs in the bath like the old ones. Do you ever stop and wonder what people are doing while they're listening to your songs? Fixing the car? Taking a dump? Getting dressed for work? Shagging? Funny that, you in the background while complete strangers are getting their end off. My daughter says she 'works out' to your record. She's sixteen now, Linda. Too old for you judging by that one in the papers last week. *She* seemed to think pretty highly of you though. 'Hung like a horse'? Shetland pony, more like. Ha-ha! Seen it in the school showers often enough. Remember when I caught you and Jonesy at it in the showers? Went back to get my trunks and there you were, Jonesy on his knees, and he wasn't playing the clarinet!

"It's all right, Buttock, your secret's safe with me. I was always good at catching people out, seeing the things they want to keep hidden. Comes in handy for the job." He lays the shirt back in the suitcase, softly singing—a pretty fair Elton John imitation, as it happens—"'*Don't let your son go down on me . . .*'"

"I wasn't a bad singer either, if I say so myself. Bloody sight better than you were anyway. I can't believe your luck, really I can't. *I* had a band for a while, you know? Of course you don't know. Why would you? We played the pubs around North London for a couple of years, got quite a big following—only local, but there was talk at one point of making a record. 'Greetings From Finsbury Park,' we were going to call it—press up a few hundred copies and flog them around the hood. But it all took too much time—rehearsals, late nights, the wives and girlfriends giving us grief. When Dawn got pregnant I chucked it in. I'm still writing songs though. I'll have to send you a tape of them, maybe you could do something with them—ha! I bet people say that to you all the time."

At the next table, a customs man is standing by an open suitcase—triumphantly, ridiculously, wielding a large salami. Its soon-to-be-ex-owner is red-faced, arguing loudly. The customs man throws his colleague a sympathetic glance.

"First thing this morning I open this case and there, stuck in a bag of dirty underwear, is this huge hunk of meat wrapped in a cloth. And it's *crawling* with maggots. And this woman nearly rips my eyes out when I say she can't bring it into the country. The traveling public is so fucking stupid. *Stupid.* You wouldn't believe what some of them try and smuggle through"—official face and matching voice —"'I'm sorry, sir, this is a serious contravention of British law under section 45 paragraph 7a of the Importation Act, now if you'll just hand it over.' And you pick up your clipboard and you turn the page and you ask for their passport and you watch the sweat break out and freeze under their eyes and you wait a while and then slowly you turn the page back and you say, 'Go on. I'll let it go this time. But *next* time . . . ,' and they grab their case and fumble with the zip like a kid caught by his mum with his willy out, and the British public is saved from the scourge of smuggling and the offending article goes into your locker, perk of the job. Like all jobs—*normal* jobs, I mean, present company excepted. You do it for forty-odd years and at the end you've got a small house and a big wife and enough in the bank for the annual jaunt to the Costa Del Sol. *You've* got a nice house. Saw it in the wife's *Hello* magazine—swimming pool, Jacuzzi. *Ja-cooooo-zee*. Big-boobed bimbos jiggling in the bubbles. Dawn keeps going on at me that she wants a Jacuzzi—one of those indoor jobs, you know, bathtubs with dog nipples all over. Gave her a fiver and told her to go get a vindaloo and fart in the bathwater, same difference.

"Yeah, I married Dawn Burchill—your old girlfriend Minerva's mate. Small, big tits—you gave her one once, re-member? She does. After a couple of drinks she tells *every-one* she's had sex with the great and glorious Spike—her mouth on your mouth, her mouth on your prick—she says you went down on her. Did you? She says, 'Why don't you go down on me like Spike?'"

A young woman has been led to the table opposite. She and the officer are both bent down over the open case, their hair almost touching. At the customs man's raised voice, they turn simultaneously and look up at Spike like Siamese twins joined at the head.

"Your parents, do they still live in Finsbury Park? Your dad, I mean—sorry about your mum, I read it in the papers. Over for the funeral I suppose. No, of course you'd have moved them to someplace more salubrious. Hah! that wouldn't be hard to find. If you thought Finsbury Park was a pit back then—well, we moved away eventually, bought a house around here. I always said I could never live in the suburbs, but anyone can live anywhere, can't they, when it comes down to it? We packed up when our youngest was born. Scarlett. Yeah, named after your song—the wife's idea. She said she wrote to you asking you to be godfather—nothing to do with me, she only told me a short while back. She said she never heard back from you. I suppose you didn't get the letter. Ha! Don't worry about it. No, seriously, I'm sure you get asked that sort of thing all the time. Letters like that probably don't even reach you. You pay people to make sure the great unwashed don't intrude on your life, don't 'invade your space,' don't pollute your pure air. What's the view like from up there, Buttock? I mean, how *do* we appear to you?"

The people from economy class crowd by with cheap suitcases piled up on trolleys. Spike hears his name muttered and whispered as they pass. His head is throbbing. It feels like a washing machine stuffed with the contents of a thousand dirty laundry bags, churning.

The customs man pulls a paperback from a corner of Spike's suitcase. He reads out the title. *"Life and How to Survive It."* He tosses it back in the case. His cheeks are livid. "Jesus H. Christ! If *you're* not satisfied, what fucking hope is there for the rest of us? You've got it all, Buttock, don't you. Living like a kid on a grown man's money—well, good luck to you, mate. Good fucking luck to you. There but for fortune. There but for one great fucking stroke of fate."

Red hands shaking, he tidies up the suitcase.

And all at once an image flashes into Spike's mind, so vivid he might have been looking at it in a magazine. It's

Knocker's bedroom. His new carpet—electric blue with red, black, and yellow swirls. His old wallpaper—"Animals of the Jungle," he remembers, and it makes him laugh. Knocker said they couldn't take it down because the British government had designated it a historic inner-city treasure. You could barely see the wall for posters anyway—Beatles, Stones, Arsenal Football Club, and that enormous map of the world he had, with the handmade flyer pinned onto America that said 'Knocker and the Dawes Tour the Universe 1965.' On a low bookcase stacked with records was the regulation one-piece, blue vinyl record player they all had. And Knocker's there on the bed, playing along to the record on his big cheap acoustic guitar, and he's on the floor, back against the wall, tapping out a rhythm on a Monopoly box lid, and Knocker's father is yelling up the stairs to keep the bloody noise down and hasn't he got a home to go to, and back home Mum's got the dinner on, the house smells of pork chops and brown sauce, and she's telling him he'd better get the table laid before his dad gets home from work. Poor Dad. Wonder how they're all holding up.

Spike reaches a hand across the table.

The customs man pulls his hand away.

"I'm all right. You don't have to lose any sleep over me. No need to lose any of your beauty fucking sleep. I'm sorry. I'm a bit tired. Had a hard week. Night shifts. Long hours. Fluorescent lights. Ultraviolet deprivation. I'm slowly crumbling, you know? The blood's slowed down. If you bumped into me now I'd crumple up like papier fucking mâché. You could turn me upside down and shake me out and I'd just be full of dust, like a vacuum cleaner bag.

"Do you want to know what's frightening, Buttock? Really fucking frightening? Watching what's happening to yourself and not being able to do a thing about it. Like those dreams where they're disemboweling you and you're paralyzed and you're watching it all going on and you know exactly what is going to happen to you but you can't move, there's not a fucking thing you can do."

The customs man rolls the numbers back around on the combination lock.

"Well, there you go then. And give my best to your old man. Spike Mattock, would you believe it? One of us made it. Bloody fucking marvelous, isn't it? It makes you feel proud. Dawn and the girls are going to get a real kick out of this when I tell them." He lifts the case down onto the floor.

"Could I have your autograph?"

# A HAPPY ENDING

"Famous for fifteen minutes?" The head of A&R was expounding into the speakerphone, something that he very much liked to do. "Fuck that, man. Everyone's gonna have their own fucking *TV* channel." Behind his back they called him BB, short for Buddha Boy, because he was young and soft and fat and had a sweet, sly smile on his baby face like he could bring you back in your next life as a prince or a peanut as soon as look at you. Which, musicbizly speaking, he could, that being the A&R man's job. Smiling benignly at the present beneficiary of his divine intervention, the Comeback Artist du jour, who was sitting upright in his chair on the other side of the enormous desk, BB leaned back in his leather swivel chair, feet on the desk-edge, swaying his hips from side to side to some private rhythm, like a fat housewife at the gym.

Cal West's dark suit, pale face, hands folded precisely in his lap, made him look more like an undertaker than a rockstar poised for a second go. He was fifty years old and looked it, except for his anxious little small-child-dropped-off-at-the-school-gates eyes. His fingers were troubling him. They felt wet and sticky, like seawater. He watched BB's hips swish forward and back like waves and a surge of seasickness rose in his throat.

There he was again—his brother, in the corner of the room, slumped up against the life-sized Springsteen promo cardboard cutout with the stars-and-stripes bandanna in the jeans back pocket. He tried looking away, but he could still see him out of the corner of his eye—grotesquely swollen, the color of cold hamburger grease, sprinkled with sand, the top part of his torso leaning out of the black body bag at an unnatural angle. His brother winked and gave him the finger.

Cal spun around, looking for his shrink, but of course he wasn't there, this was a Cal Alone Day. He tightened his grip on his fingers, which were slithering about in his lap like squids, and focused for equilibrium on a platinum album on the wall. He tried to picture what David Letterman would do. David Letterman would tug on his cuffs, relax back in his chair, drape his arm across the armrest, and smile inanely. Which is what Cal did.

He jumped as the door behind him opened. "Later, gotta go," BB said to the speakerphone. "Joel. My man. Come in." He gestured a man into his office. "We were just talking about you." Joel was a record producer, trim, tanned, of indeterminate age, with an '80s gold satin jacket and a '90s shaved head and goatee. He strode up to BB, heartily swatted his legs off the desk, and bent down and gave him a bear hug. "Looking good, man. How ya doin'!"

"I'm doin'. Joel, meet Cal. Cal, Joel. Like I've been explaining to Cal, I'm putting you guys together on this project."

Joel strode over, clasped Cal on the shoulder, and perched on the corner of the desk, blocking the cardboard Springsteen from view. Cal tried to peer around him but couldn't see anything.

"Man, I'm your biggest fan. Numero uno. I've listened to your tape, and there's some wicked shit on there. 'The Sea Sighs,' 'Dirty Orange Sky'—they're fucking ace, man. And 'The Old Man and the Sea'—that song brought tears to my eyes, I swear to God. Best thing you've done. I've got this superb rhythm section I'm working with," adding, as if he'd just that moment thought of it, "you'd be so fucking cool together. And I know an amazing keyboard guy—been on eight top fives in a row. You two would relate. You know," he said softly, "he lost a brother too—carjack down in Venice Beach, I'm not shitting you. I talked to him about working with you on your comeback and he came in his pants. He loves you."

"Did you like the song about the horses?" asked Cal. "That's my favorite. It's the first one I wrote when I came back. *'Those big strong horses sure are sweaty,'*" he sang quietly. He sounded like an angel force-fed D. H. Lawrence novels and Gauloise cigarettes. BB threw Joel a look that said that right now sweaty horses were list-topping VH1-unfriendly, and if he did like it he should unlike it, immediafuckingmente.

"Cool," Buddha Boy grinned. "We're ninety percent there, Cal. Like I said, I love what you're doing and I'm with you all the way. All it wants is to be a little bit more *now*, you know what I'm saying? What I'm seeing is a Crosby Stills and Nash-meets-Public Enemy kinda vibe, a kinda double-edged protest deal, a cry from the heart, but with *harmonies*, you got me? Not so in your face. Hard but *heart*. Your music *was* the summer. Now it's the *fall*, you know what I'm saying? You're a living legend, you've been through it, man—everybody knows what you've been through, the drugs and the breakdown and all the crazy shit—and you've come out the other end, thank God." (Not God, Cal thought. Thank

Hank, his therapist, cowriter, hairdresser, guru, his best—his only—friend. Cal Alone Days sucked donkey dick.) "And there's so many of your contemporaries who haven't, Cal, I don't need to tell you that. And everybody wants to hear all about it—they're all rooting for you out there: the critics, the public, a huge fucking demographic. They're *eager*. In this business, I can't tell you just how *sweet a sound* that is, man. This—I hate the word 'comeback'—album is gonna take you onto a whole other phase."

Cal already had his new phase figured out, and he knew what it was and he knew it was right because he'd been through so many wrong ones. It was his David Letterman phase. David Letterman, he told his shrink, is the most admired and imitated man in American culture today. He's all ego and no ego. He wears smart, dark suits and makes them look like he showered and shat in them. And word on the street is he's one of the best-endowed men in showbiz too—up there with Lyle Lovett and Tommy "T-bone" Lee. Cal bought a suit, same cut, same color, and in his visualizing sessions now he fixes on Pammie and Julia, their big shiny mouths all wet and salty, opening up for him like two great tins of sardines.

"Well, whadda you say, Cal?"

Cal was actually busy thinking. About some of his wrong phases. Like that one when he tried pretending he was pregnant, that was pretty crazy, though no crazier, as Hank pointed out to him, than a rockstar pretending to be a normal guy. He would bend over the toilet every morning with his fingers down his throat. When his sisters tried to coax him out of his bed and back into the studio he'd point at his bloated belly and shake his head. Over the years, people had made all sorts of attempts to bring him out of retirement. There was a vogue for a while of young popstars dragging all these oldies back into the limelight, like the Pet Shop Boys did with Dusty Springfield—Cal liked Dusty. There was one guy, he'd forgotten his name—he was a big hit with teenage girls in England for singing miserable songs about living in a bedsit in Manchester, although the return address, he remembered, was Chelsea, London—this guy was totally devoted to him and kept writing him letters. They were love letters, really. He said he wasn't homosexual but he'd consider having his dick cut off if Cal would make a record with him. Cal wrote him back once. "I left the business because I didn't want to be famous anymore. I found it very painful really. I really would rather be left alone and not bothered. Really I'm quite content to stay at home and just sit, or sleep mostly, which takes up quite a lot of time. Good luck. Cal." That was his bed phase, one of his all-time favorites.

So Cal said nothing, not for a long time anyway. And then finally he grinned a David Letterman grin.

"This'll amaze you—no, really." They were all attention. "Barbie is *thirty-two* years old this year. Now that makes a man feel old. Interesting fact: Placed end to end, all the Barbie dolls ever sold would circle the earth ten times. They said that about my records once—there's tens of millions of them out there. If instead of circling the earth with them you heaped 'em all up in one big pile in Southern California, Los Angeles would sink into the ocean and we'd all be drowning right now instead of sitting here talking, though the

Barbies would be all right, they'd go boob-up and float. But I guess that's talking vinyl records, though, which were a whole deal heavier than the records they make now. I made some heavy records in my time." He chuckled. "There are sixty new Barbie outfits designed each year, can you believe that? That's right, folks: time for a top ten. Number ten: Bikini Barbie—now I don't know about you but I'd find it hard to top Bikini Barbie. . . ."

BB rolled his eyes at Joel. Joel gave him a wry smile out of the left side of his mouth that said it's cool, I've seen worse, and they've gone triple platinum. BB smiled at Cal. He swung to his feet and shuffled plumply to the other side of the desk. He put one arm around Joel, the other around Cal. He gave them a big, paternal Head of A&R hug, then shooed them theatrically toward the door.

"Okay, you guys, outta here, you've got an album to make, get to fucking work. I'll come by Friday and see how you're getting on." His phone rang. "Life is tough," grimaced Buddha Boy, "ain't that the truth?"

Cal stopped on the threshold and looked him in the eye. "It's all right," he said sweetly. "I've read the book. It has a happy ending."

# LOVE STAIN

Frankie Rose died on the pavement outside the Snakehouse in Camden Town. Everywhere you went that day people would say, 'Have you heard . . . ?'—all these incomplete sentences dotting the city. Everyone was so shocked. But soon enough everyone knew that Frankie was gone, though no one could quite believe it. It was like Princess Di all over again, but a freak show Princess Di, with all these clubbers with their huge shoes, rainbow hair extensions, and clown clothes lining the streets, staying up after sunrise and paying their respects.

There was, like there always seems to be nowadays, the "amateur video" which we could all examine from the comfort of our sofas. This time it came courtesy of two young Japanese tourists. Shaky art-house footage of a slightly-built young man jerking about on his back in the street like a strobe-lit break dancer, his skull banging out a rhythm on the paving stones. Then he stopped, twitched, went rigid. His young female companion—conspicuously not his famous girlfriend Pussy, but at least dressed appropriately for the occasion in black—sat slumped against the Snakehouse wall, clutching her thin legs and staring wildly. Leo, the singer with The Nympholeptics, ran out of the club and started yelling at the bouncers to do something. They took no notice—which seemed to upset him more, to tell you the truth, than his friend's dead body. In the three weeks since Frankie had got him his record deal, Leo was already getting used to people doing what he said.

Then the camcorder jerked around and we saw a tiny Japanese woman with little-girl pigtails, spotted miniskirt, hooped leggings, and platform trainers standing next to Frankie's body, waving and giggling shyly. She went up close to the lens and everything went fuzzy. Then came a skinny Japanese man with dyed yellow hair and voluminous combat trousers, posing coolly in front of the Snakehouse sign. Then, for no apparent reason, the camera swung out toward the road and stopped for a few moments on a pair of baby's bootees hanging on a car's rearview mirror, before lurching drunkenly back to Frankie's corpse and the people coming out of the club down the road—stepping over him, not bothering to look down, like he was just another of the countless losers lying in the street in Camden Town.

A car drove past, stopped, and someone took a picture out of the window. A strange still life it must have made: the curious Japanese couple, the girl slumped against the wall, the body lying face-up on the ground, a bouncer and assorted musicians leaning over him, the drummer still clutching his sticks in a V in one hand. An ambulance wailed down the High Street, weaving past the double-parked minicabs, a police car hugging its behind.

Overnight, the spot where Frankie fell became a shrine. Then it became a party. At first it was small clutches of clubbers, teary-eyed girls and guys leaving bouquets and cards they'd bought at late-night rock 'n' roll Sainsbury's, but by morning it had become a torrent. The Northern Line was jammed. The High Street was impassable, a solid mass of people and flowers from Camden to Mornington Crescent tube: cars hooting, people waving out of windows, kids with boom boxes sitting cross-legged on the pavement listening to pirate radio cranking out the beats, calling friends on their mobiles telling them to come down and join them. The police tried to move them on but pretty soon, through sheer force of numbers, they had to give up. Success made people heady and all around you could see them dancing and hugging, sharing Class As and alcopops, as the music got louder and the pavement shimmered like the desert in the hottest summer in London in years.

In front of the Snakehouse the first to arrive had staked out their territory and were guarding it as fiercely as any cat. Top real estate were the four paving slabs that Frankie Rose had puked on, where some hard-core girls were holding vigil and picking out, like nightclub bouncers, who would or wouldn't be allowed to get close enough to look. Hawkers were already squeezing through the crowd selling souvenir posters with a photo of the Sacred Paving Stones; the words 'Love Stain' were written below in cutout Sex Pistoly letters in the style of Frankie's last album sleeve.

Those people who accuse Britain of lacking enterprise can't have seen the speed with which they got the Dead Frankie merchandise out on the streets. Gone were the usual imitation sixties Indian tat, the fake Afghan jackets and velvet loons, and in came the Frankie mugs and prayer rugs and iconic T-shirts and those great souvenir pens that you held upside down and Frankie's baggy trousers fell off. By the end of the week there were already three new Frankie Rose biographies in the shops. It made you wonder: Were there really people who could write 75,000 words in less than forty-eight hours, or had the authors got a library of celebrity books ready and waiting on the outside chance one of them might pop off? Or maybe the three of them had got together and hatched a plot to kill Frankie and rake it in. Now, that was one the conspiracy theorists hadn't come up with yet.

Though a quick trawl through Google uncovered just about everything else. There were no end of Murder vs. Accidental Overdose debates—the majority opting for the former, with Pussy and Leo Nympholeptic heading the list of suspects. Although Frankie wasn't really dead, of course, he just wanted to get away from Pussy/Leo/the music business, and right now he's living in Tuscany/Switzerland/the Australian outback/backpacking with hippies in Peru. Frankie had been spotted in the frozen food section at Ralphs Supermarket in Hollywood and in the baked goods department of Waitrose on Holloway Road—first instance alone, second accompanied by five men dressed like Reservoir Dogs. Someone claimed to have accosted Frankie in the duty-free shop on the Dover-Calais ferry and told him he owed it to his fans to go home. Several girls in several locations several thousand miles apart claimed they'd spent the previous night shagging him and said we would believe them in nine months' time.

I printed off a page from the KillEmAll site, which offered helpful instructions on how to top yourself in the exact same way as your favorite star. Right above Kurt Cobain (quantity of heroin; size and gauge of shotgun; where to lie down; head position; angle of shooting arm) and Mama Cass (precise ham sandwich recipe) I found Frankie Rose and the formula for "John Belushis"—cocaine and heroin speedballs, apparently his drug of choice. When I ran into Leo Nympholeptic at the Underworld a fortnight later, it looked like Frankie had bequeathed him his drug dealer. He was staggering about the place, bumping into people—girls mostly, I noticed—before heading for the bar at the back. He was staring at himself in the mirror when I dragged over a stool and sat down next to him. When he saw my reflection he said, "You're a journalist, aren't you. I saw you taking notes."

"You caught me out." I smiled.

"Who're you writing about?" He swung around on the stool and looked at me, or to be more precise at my breasts—first the left, then the right, then the left one again, like I was Wimbledon.

"You," I said, and then *he* smiled. I made some small talk about his band and where they were playing next, then slipped in the subject of the night they played Snakehouse. He gave a blow-by-blow account of The Nympholeptics' triumphant performance, not mentioning Frankie once. I told him I met someone who said he'd seen Frankie in the men's room while The Nympholeptics were onstage. He was leaning over the filthy urinal, head rested on the smeared white tiles like he was in pain, and staring at a frayed wet butt-end floating in a puddle of piss. The guy had asked him if he was all right and Frankie said "Sure," stood straight upright, and strolled back into the club.

Leo looked me in the eyes. "None of those mother-fuckers know nothing about Frankie. *Nothing.*" But you do, I said gently. He looked away. I asked him if he'd put the record straight but he answered, "I don't want to talk about it." I wrote down my phone number and told him to call if he changed his mind and that I was serious about doing a story on him and The Nympholeptics. There was a message from him on my answering machine when I got home.

Leo's flat was above a dry cleaner's off the Seven Sisters Road. A social security–style bedsit with bumpy wood-chip wallpaper painted shiny cream, like baby-sick. There was a bed with a filthy pink velvet headboard and a filthier Playboy quilt cover, a cheap white laminated chest of drawers, a table, and an unfolded folding chair, all of them with their edges chewed off. There was a clump of brown wilted organic matter in a pot on the windowsill that might have been a spider plant once before a combination of neglect and dry-cleaning fumes became too much to bear. Not a huge record company advance, then.

I sat down on the chair by the open window. It was uncomfortably hot. The air, outside and in, was rancid—a thick, cheesy mix of car fumes, armpits, dry-cleaning fluid, burnt rubber, and piss-dipped cotton-wool.

"Want some tea?" Leo asked. He was wearing a stained T-shirt that might possibly once have been white.

"Thanks," I said.

"If I make you a cup will you show me your tits?" He smirked as he dug a mug out of the sink, tipped out what appeared to be plankton, and held it for a moment or two under the gas heater spout. As the kettle boiled, he took a carton of milk and a can of Special Brew out of the fridge. "Last one," he said, snapping back the ring-pull and taking a slug while dunking my teabag in the water. The more he dunked, the more his face clouded over.

"I think," he said, finally fishing out the teabag with his fingers and chucking it in the sink, "that it is very possible that Frankie was killed."

"What do you mean?"

He handed me the mug and looked at my tape recorder. "Is that thing off?" Frankie had obviously taught him a trick or two about interviews.

"It is if you want it to be," I said.

He watched me push the button, then went over and sat on the bed with his beer. And started to tell me a strange—well, ridiculous—story.

"Frankie's manager, Clive MacFee, once used to manage this decrepit old motherfucker name of Perry Kaye—you heard of him? Had a bunch of hits in the early eighties but hadn't done shit in years. Kaye, so MacFee told Frankie, was giving him a hard time about getting him some gigs or something, but like MacFee said, what the motherfuck can you do with these old farts except stick 'em on them cheap Christmas nostalgia compilations and trot em out for awards shows?"

Leo raised his right buttock. I braced myself for an additional room fragrance but instead he excavated a squashed pack of Camels from his back pocket. When his attempts to coolly tap a cigarette through a hole in the top corner failed, he ripped the packet open, taking out what looked like a small, sad, sculptural representation of a Greek letter S. Straightening it out as best he could, he lit it with a Zippo.

"Where was I?"

"Awards shows."

"Right, MacFee told Frankie about this show he was at where Kaye was doing some kind of god-awful greatest hits medley, and MacFee and this bloke from Kaye's record company were watching him on a monitor in the green room. Both of them were shaking their heads. 'They should be forced to retire at fifty,' said MacFee, 'like in the army.'

"'Better still,' said the record company bloke, 'shoot 'em. There's nothing does more for record sales than death.'

'Can't argue there,' says MacFee. 'Look what it did for Lennon. That comeback album of his was a *dog*. Wouldn't have shifted shit if it wasn't for that mad cunt with the gun.'

"The record company bloke held up his glass and made a toast. 'To Mark David Chapman.' 'Mark David Chapman.' MacFee bashed his glass. They were laughing, but the thought is obviously niggling at MacFee because later he starts getting obsessed with dreaming up all these different ways of killing Perry Kaye off. He told Frankie all this crazy shit he'd tried. Like the photo session on the White Cliffs of Dover with the photographer going, 'Back just a touch, Perry—just a little more.' Or the pair of antique pistols MacFee bought Kaye for his birthday that nearly blew the cleaning lady's head off when she was dusting them."

"It was a joke," I said. "He was taking the piss."

"Judging by what happened to Kaye *and* to Frankie, I know what I think. Kaye died while making the video for 'Catch Me I'm Falling,' right? The stuntman doesn't show up; the video director has a motherfucking fit and threatens to charge double if he has to reshoot; the young blonde who's meant to be his love interest is staring at his Elton John hair weave like she's about to toss her cookies. So next thing you know Kaye is up in the plane, jumping. The chute doesn't open. And his last album, a masterpiece of motherfucking scrofulosity, suddenly soars to number one."

"So that's it then. The manager did it."

"All I'm saying is it's too coincidental to be a coincidence."

"But why kill Frankie? What doesn't fit is Frankie wasn't past it. Everything he touched topped the charts. Everyone loved Frankie." Except Frankie. Frankie could have captained the Olympics self-hate team. That throat infection that made him cancel that last tour? MacFee got a call from him at four in the morning and rushed round to find his star strung out and naked—strung up too, a belt around his neck fixed to the top of the door, and gripping his dick and crying like an abandoned baby. He told MacFee he wanted out.

"What you don't know," said Leo, after a pause, "is that Frankie wanted out."

"From what?"

"I'll tell you from what," though he doesn't. He changes the subject, "Do you want to know what *really* motherfucks me off? It's that shit going round that the whole thing was staged."

"Sorry?"

"You know, that it was a put-up job and he's still alive. What they're saying, right, is that Frankie, who is now in the back of an ambulance screaming down Camden High Street, has to unzip the body bag from the inside, rustle up a look-alike, jump out of the ambulance at fifty miles an hour without anyone seeing him, and disappear."

"You mean disappear like his girlfriend Pussy did."

"Motherfuck!" He rescued the last squashed cigarette from the packet, lit it, and fell back onto the bed, dragging on it furiously. He lay there for a while kicking his heels, glaring at the ceiling. The traffic appeared to have stopped for the moment and the room was quiet, aside from the chug and whir of the dry-cleaning machines downstairs.

Leo finally broke the silence. "I mean," he said slowly, like he was figuring the whole thing out as he went along, "let's just say that in theory that the first bit could have happened—the ambulance might have hit a hole in the road, the jolt might have kick-started Frankie's heart, and he opens his eyes, sees where he is, and decides to get the motherfuck out. I accept that is possible. But *disappear*? Someone like Frankie can't disappear. I mean, *I* could disappear. It would be tough," he added quickly as his new musician-with-a-record-deal ego kicked in, "but Frankie's the biggest rockstar in the country. And anyway, if he had've disappeared, I'd know about it. I mean I'm his best motherfucking mate."

That's why Frankie was at The Nympholeptics' show. That's why The Nympholeptics had a record deal.

"Face it, Frankie's dead. End of interview. Now," he said, springing up from his horizontal position and onto the edge of the bed, "do I get to see your tits?"

"No, the tea was shit, but thanks for asking."

"Fair enough," he said shrugging. "Any chance of a cover story?"

That was over ten months ago. Frankie hasn't surfaced, nor for that matter have any of his rumored offspring, and Clive MacFee is now managing Leo's band. Their first single, "My Best Friend," is due out on the anniversary of Frankie Rose's death. MacFee bought the rights to the Japanese couple's camcorder film for their video.

The Snakehouse is all boarded up now—after a couple of drug raids the authorities closed it down. But the girls are still there, every day, rain or shine, blagging cash from the tourists who want to take their picture and mandating whose photos and trinkets and love letters will be stapled to the heaving front door. The Love Stain is still there too. Probably always will be. Camden Council is notoriously crap at cleaning up.

# RHINESTONE TOMBSTONE BLUES

LeeAnn Starmountain was sitting in front of the window in her favorite writing chair when the phone call came to say her mother was dead.

She had, as it happens, been plotting ways to kill her at the very moment the phone rang. This was nothing unusual for LeeAnn. It had ceased by this stage to be anything personal. It was her way of relaxing, like doing crossword puzzles might be for other folk. A ritual that helped free up her imagination to write songs. She couldn't even say she hated her mother anymore; at least she couldn't summon up the actual emotions. She just accepted that she did and took it from there. Some of the sweetest, most plaintive love songs that LeeAnn ever wrote started life with her mother's head severed by a falling stained-glass window, or a cannibal preacher stir-frying her heart, or her mother pinned and slowly bleeding beneath the wheels of a semitruck with a "Jesus Saves" bumper sticker and LeeAnn in the passenger seat giving the driver the blow job of his life.

By now, over the course of the two hundred seventeen songs she had written, sixty of which had made the country music charts, eight of them at number one, LeeAnn reckoned she'd come up with every conceivable way there was of dispatching her mother to the Happy Homestead in the Sky where the angels wear high-necked nighties and their breath smells of apple pie. Which is why, all the while that her tearful sister Beth was relating how Mom had been baked alive by her electric blanket, slowly, over the course of a week, LeeAnn felt not so much shocked or sorrowful or horrified or bereaved as resentful. The whole time she was mouthing her oh-my-Gods she was thinking of her mother lying paralyzed by a stroke on her bed, marinating in her own urine, staring night after night at that framed picture of Jesus Christ on the bedroom wall that looked like Brad Pitt in *Legends of the Fall*, and slow-cooking to perfection.

It was just like her to go come up with something LeeAnn hadn't thought of yet. It was as if her mother had deprived her of the perfect, and now never-to-be-written, song.

When she hung up she was shaking; she could have used a drink, but there was nothing in the house, hadn't been since she graduated summa cum laude from Betty Ford's. She went to the bathroom, leaned over the basin, and stared at herself in the mirror for a long time, as if confirming she was still there. She looked older. Maybe it was because she no longer had a mother to measure herself against. She could see the headline above the face in the mirror: "Bizarre Death: The Heartbreak Behind the Glamour of Country's Hottest Star."

The phone rang again. Her answering machine kicked in. She heard the businesslike voice of her manager, Ross Silver, telling her he'd just gotten off the phone with Todd Tamara—Todd managed the heavy metal group Shoot 2 Kill, the biggest-selling band in the States, who'd spent twelve weeks at number one with their version of her country ballad "Sweet Summer Breeze"; she wound up doing an interview with their singer, Rex, on KLIT, the Los Angeles metal radio station. Distracted for a moment, LeeAnn pictured Rex's taut twenty-five-year-old body in its trademark tiny tight white shorts. Ross was telling her machine that Todd reckoned Rex was planning to split and go solo and he wanted to get together with LeeAnn and collaborate on some songs.

The phone rang again. "Hi, Miss Starmountain? It's Josh Harris, from *Hats the Way I Like It* in Atlanta"—*Hats* was one of the young, hip New Traditionalist magazines that had sprouted like mushrooms since the latest country music boom. The voice was respectful but resolute. "We've just heard a report that your mother has passed on in, uh, unusual circumstances? First of all, ma'am, our sincere condolences on your tragedy, and my apologies for calling you at home at such a time, but as soon as we heard, we pulled the front page of the March issue and we want to put you on the cover instead, and of course we're working a pretty tight deadline here now, so if we could just get a few words? I've left a message with your manager. Anyhow, I'll keep trying till I get ahold of you. Thank you kindly, Miss Starmountain, and once again, my deepest sympathy on your tragic loss."

As soon as he hung up, it rang once more. It was Ross Silver again. "LeeAnn. LeeAnn?" This time there was an odd catch in his voice. "I know you're there, darling, I've been trying your cell phone, please pick up the phone. Jesus, LeeAnn, I just found out—some jerk of a journalist from *Brats in Hats* or *Saps in Chaps* or whatever the fuck that magazine is called left a message on my voice mail just now while I was on the line to you. I called the police to check it out. Look, LeeAnn, stay where you are, don't move, I'm coming over. Love you, darling. I'll be right there." After a brief beep, the phone rang again. She heard her cell phone trilling a quiet background accompaniment from the kitchen table where she'd left it. She ignored them both, and stayed staring at the mirror, past the surface of her face and into the lines, recently plumped out with collagen, which now looked deeply corrugated and so disconnected somehow from the rest of her that LeeAnn felt sorry for them. And finally she cried.

She cried even harder on the flight back home. The cute young steward in first class, who crouched by her seat and solicitously held her hand, and the sweet blonde stewardess who leaned over and dabbed triangular white damask napkins at the mascara rivulets trickling below her dark glasses, figured, as they would have, that she was weeping for her mother, but LeeAnn was weeping for herself. She did not want to go but her manager said she had to. "LeeAnn," he said, "I know how you feel, but your country audience is not going to understand if you don't. For Christ's sake, LeeAnn, she may have been a Bible-bashing child-abusing bitch but she's your mother. And anyhow, don't you want to make sure that she really is dead? I'm not saying you have to stick around and sing at the memorial service—although come to think of it that's not such a bad idea; shame it's not summer or we could have maybe done some kind of outdoors tribute concert. . . ." Her ex-husband, the country singer "Big" Willie Bean, had left a message on her machine just a few moments before, suggesting the very same thing and volunteering his support, onstage and off.

She could just picture it: a giant photograph of Mother on the video screens, LeeAnn and Willie Bean in matching fringed white jackets with black sparkly armbands, his arm tight around her, she weeping on his shoulder, back together, united in grief, on her new song, "Rhinestone Tombstone Blues." Maybe they could turn it into one of those county fairs with an outside barbecue—hot roasted Momma, straight off the spit, just a dollar fifty. "The media are going to go for a story like this like vultures," said Silver. "If you give them the chance, LeeAnn, they'll rip you apart."

A couple of dozen photographers and some TV news cameras were there to meet her when she landed. So was Beth, her favorite sister if she had to choose one, all creasy-eyed and anxious. Her big, stiff, lacquered hair looked out of proportion with her small, droopy face. Four other sisters were at home with their father, the seventh had just boarded a flight out of England. Beth hugged LeeAnn as the cameras flashed—self-consciously, as if she were the winner of a "Dream Date With" contest. They didn't say anything. LeeAnn gripped Beth's hand, her long red nails gouging half-moons in her flesh, and together the two women walked solemnly to the exit through the path the airport staff cleared.

Home was an hour's drive away, and as Beth re-laxed behind the wheel, the barriers came down. She talked nonstop—about their father, about the funeral arrangements, who was coming, the coroner's report, all the minutiae of their mother's death. She talked about her kids and her husband and her sisters' kids and husbands, brought her up-to-date on where they were all living and who was doing what. She told her how incredulous and then proud her oldest boy had been when she told him his aunt wrote a song for Shoot 2 Kill, his number one band.

As they drove through their hometown, Beth—who really should have been a gossip columnist; back less than one day and she'd already found out everything worth knowing—pointed out to LeeAnn what had changed and what had stayed the same. Doreen Swensen had been cured and let out of the madhouse; she was helping out at her cousin's hardware store and now she could hold a screwdriver, "allegedly," without using it on some girl's eyeballs. The guy who ran the pharmacy had been jailed last year for swallowing the entire contents of the place and running down Main Street with his dick out. Barbie, who was in LeeAnn's class, came back from New York with an out-of-work actor who can't be more than half her age and they bought old Proctor's place up on Vermont. The son-of-son-of-son-of Sex Dog—his great-grandfather, a horny Airedale-retriever mix they used to call Sex Dog, would terrify the sisters with his attentions when they were young—had had to be put down when he tried to mount the deputy sheriff's baby boy. Lorrie Phillips, who owned the diner and was once LeeAnn's boss, married a young guy from the religious right that she met on the Internet; they set up a website, Hymens4Heaven.com, to save young girls' sexuality for the Lord. Their last posting—before the church put a stop to it—recommended anal sex as a means of preserving a girl's virginity: "Be a virgin in front and a martyr behind," said a bubble coming out of a picture of Lorrie's zealous, smiling face, "and the angels will sound their horns on high." The diner closed down long ago, the fast-food chains had taken over.

Within a two-block space LeeAnn counted a Carl's Jr., a Bob's Big Boy, a Top Burger, and a big, gleaming new drive-thru McDonald's. "On opening day," Beth said, swinging onto tree-lined Richmond Avenue, "they ran a photograph of its first customer in the local newspaper. Who do you think it was? Tommy Moorhead! He looked *awful.* There's a man if ever I saw one with grounds for a lawsuit against God. And they ran this little interview with him where he told them who he was—who he was married to, in other words—and he stunned them all, reeling off all these fascinating facts about McDonald's, how it opened on April fifteenth, 1955, in Des Plaines, Illinois, the Chicago suburb now 'better known as Burger Bethlehem,' I quote your exhusband, and how the first Big Macs were fifteen cents but *he* only ever ordered Chicken McNuggets, because he was, in his own words, 'an individual.' I am so *sure.*"

They were still laughing when Beth pulled into the forecourt of the Chapel of Rest. They stopped abruptly, looked at each other uncomfortably. The ease and familiarity seemed to have been switched off with the engine. "You go ahead," Beth said. "I have to go to the office and call the others and tell them we're here." LeeAnn fumbled in her handbag for her cell phone. "Here, use this," she said awkwardly, proffering it to her sister.

"You do it. I don't know how to use those things."

"I don't know the number," said LeeAnn pathetically. Her sister tutted and sighed.

"It's been the same one for forty years." She recited the numbers and LeeAnn pushed the buttons. When she heard one of her sisters answer, she thrust the phone at Beth. Beth glared at her. "Hi, Ruthie," LeeAnn said. "We've just gotten to the chapel." States of well-being were checked and arrangements were made. "Ruthie says they'll all be here in fifteen minutes. Except for Evangeline, who's staying home with Pop."

"How *is* Pop?" LeeAnn asked for the first time. "How the hell do you think?" said Beth, still angry though she couldn't for sure say why. "The one blessing is I don't think he even knows what's going on. No need to do that," she said as LeeAnn automatically checked that her door was locked. "We're in God's country now."

"And He's fucking welcome to it ," muttered LeeAnn under her breath.

The Chapel of Rest was wood-paneled, cool and spacious, and dimly lit, with a few tasteful china ornaments dotted about. It reminded LeeAnn of the stately home that she visited with "Big" Willie Bean when they were in England together on tour. Only the stately home didn't have a fucking great coffin in the middle of the room. She knew she had to look in it sooner or later, she just preferred later. LeeAnn stayed glued to the reproduction antique chair while Beth stood over the coffin, stroking something—she guessed it was their mother's hair—talking softly to whatever was in it, and whatever was in it LeeAnn really did not want to know.

A wave of nausea rolled up in her solar plexus. She hadn't felt this sick since she was twelve weeks pregnant with Tommy Moorhead's baby, the baby she aborted the second she ran off to L.A. and the butchers fucked up her insides so bad there was no way she would ever get morning sickness again. But it sure felt like it now. Figuring this was not the best spot to recycle her airline food, even if it was first-class airline food, LeeAnn stood up. The nausea drained to the floor. She walked over to Beth, wobbling like her legs were made of Play-Doh, and stood behind her sister, her hands on her shoulders. She felt Beth sob. But still LeeAnn didn't look down. Her sisters arrived, came over and hugged her, bent down into the coffin and kissed their mother, rearranged her hair and dress, trying to make her nice, like she was their little girl whom they were getting ready for a party and not 140 pounds of God-fearing, stick-wielding, Bible-quoting, burnt old meat.

This *thing*—LeeAnn still didn't look down—once ruled their lives with terror and turned their father into a pitiful wreck long before the Alzheimer's finished off the job. She used to line the girls up, kneel them all down in a row, and if the hems of their skirts failed to brush the ground she'd beat them. She'd make them recite the Scriptures and if they got one word wrong she'd beat them. She'd make surprise raids on their bedrooms in the middle of the night to see what they were up to and, whatever they were up to, she'd beat them. LeeAnn got the worst of it, being the oldest and an example and all. When LeeAnn's first period started, and she was scared shitless and hurting, and had no idea what was going on, and after two days finally got up the nerve to tell her mom she was bleeding, she beat her stupid. She was a woman now, her mother said, so she had better get on her knees and pray to God. Menstruation was God's monthly reminder that a woman's body is a piece of dirt that must be cleansed by the blood of Jesus, until her husband purifies it with the gift of birth. A woman's body, she said, belongs to her husband and her soul belongs to God. Then her mother left her praying and went out. Fifteen minutes later she threw a packet of thick white pads and an elastic belt on her bed.

LeeAnn was surprised to find herself trembling. This is crazy, she thought, being scared of a goddam shish kabob. And finally she looked down.

It was both better and worse than she'd expected. Her mother looked like a voodoo doll that someone had dressed up in their grandma's Sunday best. Like one hell of a slab of jerky. Like a strange effigy made out of dried brown animal skin by some Indian tribe with an arts grant. She looked smaller than she expected too—reduced, like a shrunken head. But she was still utterly terrifying. LeeAnn gingerly lifted her mother's thin, leather hand. Someone had taped her worn-out old wedding ring to what remained of her finger. LeeAnn thought of the song she wrote for her third husband, Lee Starmountain, the only one she'd really loved. "'He wore out his wedding ring,'" she sang gently to herself, like a lullaby "'on the steering wheel,'" and hot tears plopped into the coffin.

The women piled into two cars and went back to the house. Evangeline was at the door before they'd even pulled up. She'd been out watching the local cops get the press and TV video crews to move back to the other side of the street. There were still some people milling around outside—local women mostly, middle-aged, in leisure clothes with gold appliqué flowers and animals and incongruously teased hair—hoping to get a look at their prodigal star. Some of them, unashamed, had cameras poised and ready. Others waved and said, "Hi, LeeAnn. Welcome home." She gave them the barest acknowledgment and went inside with her sisters.

The place was much as she remembered. Stifling, claustrophobic. Knickknacks everywhere, kitschy decorations, crosses in every shape and size and substance. Hanging china plates with homilies and verses from the Bible lined the walls. Her grandmother's framed sampler, "As Ye Sow So Shall Ye Reap," took pride of place above the fireplace where the mirror ought to have been, only Mom would not allow a mirror in the house. Even now LeeAnn retained her ability to put on her makeup without one. In spite of all their cleaning, the place did not smell good. Evangeline gestured upstairs and said that Rick from the garage was coming by later with his pickup to take the mattress away. The police had offered, but their father had refused to let it go. Maybe he was sentimental. Maybe just mental. Maybe he wanted to worship it as the one thing on this earth that had ever shut her up. He didn't say. He couldn't say. Then again, he never could.

"How long are you staying?" Evangeline asked her in the kitchen as she helped with the dishes. "I'm going back tonight," said LeeAnn.

"Tonight? What about the funeral?"

"I'll fly back again," said LeeAnn. Adding, suddenly conscious of such a display of conspicuous consumption in the family home, "I've got some commitments. Work. You know. I can't stay." They carried on in silence.

It was just before she left for the airport, while the taxi purred outside the front door, that Evangeline took her to one side and gave her the envelope. She'd found it in her mother's dresser drawer while she was going through her things. It was a plain white eight-by-four with "For LeeAnn Moorhead, in case of my death" written neatly on it—her married name, her first marriage, the only one her mother recognized. "You know, Mother was really fond of you," Evangeline confided. LeeAnn snorted. "I know it wasn't always easy, but maybe—" LeeAnn stood there silent, dumb, clutching the letter. "I guess she felt she had something she needed to say to you," said Evangeline sweetly. "You know, maybe make up?" LeeAnn stuffed the envelope into her bag. They went back and joined the others. She kissed them all good-bye—all except her father; she couldn't; he just sat there staring and dribbling like a dirty old man on a park bench—and then she was out of there.

Sitting in the cab, the house and then the town disappearing into the distance, she should have felt like all the weight in the world had lifted from her shoulders, but the tiny envelope in her handbag weighed her down. She held the bag closed tightly on her lap. She wanted to know what was in it and she didn't. So maybe her mother wanted to "make up"—well, hooray for her—go meet her maker with a nice, easy conscience and with a few words Wite-Out and rewrite LeeAnn's whole existence. Maybe it was a declaration of love. Hell, that would be worse than eternal hatred; at least with that she knew where she stood. A sharp, unexpected pang stabbed LeeAnn in the stomach. It was, she knew, a ridiculous longing to make up. She wanted to throw the goddamn letter out of the taxi window, but it felt too heavy to lift from the bag. She didn't know how she managed to carry her ten-ton handbag all the way to the airport departure gate.

In a first-class seat twenty thousand miles up and twenty minutes from landing, LeeAnn finally felt safe enough to open it. Inside was a single sheet of white paper the size of a leaflet folded, very neatly, in half. Trembling in spite of herself, LeeAnn opened it out. She read the dozen words written in her mother's bold but spidery handwriting. She dropped it to the floor. It was lying in the aisle when the stewardess passed. She picked it up and held it out to LeeAnn. "No," said LeeAnn, shaking her head, "it's nothing to do with me," and the stewardess took it away.

The bar was empty but for the barman. She hadn't been in the Lucky Shamrock for over a year, but he greeted her like a regular. "I want you to take down every bottle you've got on that shelf up there," said LeeAnn, "and pour it all in one glass, and then pour another for yourself. I'm celebrating."

"What's the occasion?" said the barman.

"Leaving home," said LeeAnn. The cell phone rang. She jumped; she thought it was still turned off. She switched it to message mode. Her manager had already left a dozen messages since she stepped off the plane. "How did it go, darling?" "LeeAnn, call me." "Call me as soon as you get this." "LeeAnn, this is very urgent." He said he'd set up an interview on *Good Morning America* for tomorrow, 8 A.M. "Big" Willie Bean was serious about the memorial concert. Nashville was proposing a TV special. *Us* magazine wanted to do the funeral, and was offering a cover.

The barman brought her glass. She raised it up. "I want to make a toast. To God," she said, "and the Lord Jesus Christ and all his happy little helpers," and downed the drink in one. "To God," said the barman, and took a sip from his glass. "Same again, young man," said LeeAnn, slapping her glass down on the bartop. The barman carried another drink over. Again she knocked it straight back. "What do you say we make it a nice round three?" LeeAnn laughed. The alcohol was kicking in fast. She pointed to a bottle on the top shelf: "And you might add a little of that pretty blue one this time."

"One Latino-Russian Surprise with a dash of curaçao it is." He handed her the multicolored concoction. She held it up to the light, admiring its swirling beauty. The barman figured she was making another toast and lifted his glass again. "Who's this one to?" he asked.

"To my mother," said LeeAnn, slurring only very slightly. "A toast for my toasted mom. And to her very last gift to her firstborn baby girl."

"And what was that?" asked the barman.

"Oh, just a little old letter." Her face had drained of color, but her cheeks were livid. "Something my mother wanted to tell me." The barman raised his eyebrows expectantly.

LeeAnn emptied her glass, "She said, 'LeeAnn, THERE IS NO FIRE ESCAPE IN HELL. Don't you ever forget that.'" Holding the cool glass against her cheeks, her voice was stone-cold sober. "Don't worry, Momma, I won't."

# CLOSE TO YOU (COVER SONG)

It all began in an old building in Kentish Town, a nondescript end-of-terrace whose ground floor, until it caught fire, was occupied by a kabob take-away. The upstairs floors were roasted along with it, as well as the mad old Greek woman who lived there but spent most of her time ranting outside the orthodox church over the road. The place just sat there for a while, empty, scorched paint flaking off the dirty cream side wall, while the authorities decided whether to do it up or pull it down.

Then one day, another old Greek lady on her way to the church glanced up to where her unfortunate comrade had met her end, and all at once fell to her knees, clutching her bosom. A face had appeared on the wall. A gaunt, pale, melancholic face with a kind, gentle smile.

*It was Jesus Christ.*

A passerby came over thinking it was a heart attack, but all the old lady could do was point at the wall and wail. After a while people came out of the shops to see what the racket was about. Before long they were joined by a TV crew. After that the kabob Jesus was everywhere. Whenever the Council sent builders over to try to start work on the place, they were seen off by worshippers. A couple of times a scuffle broke out. Every day a bit more of the figure would appear in the paintwork—the long, serene, modest face with its gently closed eyelids and dark, wavy hair falling over a pale, bony sternum. And over a firm pair of breasts.

It quickly became apparent that it was not Jesus at all. That it wasn't even a man. Who it was—as any music fan could have told you; the likeness was astounding—was Karen Carpenter.

Since she had chosen to make her first known apparition in my scuzzy little neighborhood, it was only polite to write something about it. "Karen starved for us," my piece concluded, "so it is right and fitting that she should choose this kabobbery, this shrine to fat, as her temple. Like the lamb on the spit, she turned in the flames of celebrity, becoming in the process thinner and thinner as her fans grabbed their pound of flesh."

"Karen did not die for you, you sad, dysfunctional bitch," read the e-mail. "Karen would not have even SHAT ON YOUR SHOES. Richard has maintained a DIGNIFIED SILENCE and it would be a BETTER THING FOR THE WORLD if you did too." The return address was thekarenclub @aol.com. I guess I must have upset someone.

A day or two later it must have been, I was walking past the old take-away and I noticed there were people inside. There were blankets hung up over the cracked windows, but through the gap you could see mattresses and sleeping bags on the floor. Squatters. After a week or so, when it became clear that no one was going to bother to evict them, they would leave the front door open while they tried to clean the place up. "We've only just begun," a honey voice glided out of the portable CD player, "to live." They weren't the usual squatters you got around here. All of them were women, most of them mumsy, several middle-aged, dressed in prim smart-casuals and with a nice smile for anyone who passed. At some point the broken glass was replaced and I could see that they'd done a remarkable job. They'd even restored the old tiled food counter and found a replacement for the curved, translucent Perspex lid that covered the entire length of the refrigerated section where the chef used to keep the trimmings. Then they put up some flouncy floral curtains, so I couldn't see in anymore. But occasionally, when the noise of the traffic was not too loud, you could hear a pure sad voice keening about rainy days and Mondays getting her down.

First I'd figured they were planning to open some kind of café—but with the state of the building, it would have had to have been an unofficial one, and these women looked too respectable for anything like that. Maybe they were setting up a soup kitchen for the homeless. Then one day a sign appeared on the curtained front door. It read, "The Karen Club." I knocked on the door—tentatively; I hadn't forgotten that e-mail—and someone peered around the curtains. They didn't let me in.

In the weeks that followed, there was an outbreak of Karen sightings across the globe: in Berlin, on a small remaining section of the Wall; in a Tokyo shopping mall (initially claimed by some young fans as an apparition of Edward Van Halen); on the Greek island of Lesbos (although most people suspected this one was a put-up job); and in Tampa, Florida—the biggest Karen so far, the entire flank of a multistory bank building. Each of them became a magnet to the kind of women who don't tend to gather in communal situations, unless it's church socials or Barry Manilow concerts. And they all adopted the same name: "The Karen Club."

To look at them, they were harmless enough. No more or less obsessive than young men who paint their faces to look like dragons, cats, and spacemen and go to see KISS. But the brutality with which the elders fought for their own clique's position as the chosen church of Karen, the underhanded tactics—the art restorers sneaking in at night to make subtle improvements to the image; the checks the wealthy divorcées sent to Karen's brother (all of them returned) in the hope of buying his support; the private detectives hired to get the dirt on the leaders of the rival Karen Clubs—all made it pretty clear that these women weren't to be messed with.

In the lower ranks there was some interfaction squabbling, but it was mostly confined to the message boards: "This is SO not in the spirit of Karen," someone or other would write somewhere—but no one had quite agreed what the spirit of Karen should be. The Americans and Australians seemed to focus on homemaking, low-fat recipes, and working out. The Japanese were into merchandise. The Lesbos franchise seemed to have better things to do than spend too much time online. And the Germans were heavily into analyzing the meaning of the lyrics—" 'Calling Occupants of Interplanetary Craft': proof of extraterrestrial life or divine prophecy?"—and exploring the Antigone myth.

"What if her brother had been her lover?" posed one club member.

"You are one WEIRD SICKO," came the answer. "And anyhow if he had it would not have been the same."

"Downey, California," another replied, "is not Ancient Greece."

"Ah, but remember, the London Karen," wrote a British visitor to the Berlin site, "WAS first discovered by an ancient Greek."

"Don't mention those BLASPHEMERS," wrote someone else.

The Kentish Town branch had changed its name, on its door and website, to the High Kathedral of Karen. Its members were talking about organizing a synod, bringing in Karen Club reps from across the world for a Sacred Grilling. They invited the press—a little party with canapés and white wine, the stereo playing "Solitaire" and "Superstar" and "Sweet Sweet Smile"—and the three leaders gave a short speech. Then they turned up the volume and turned on the halogen lights above the refrigerated counter. A dark shape became visible under the translucent curved cover. The oldest member of the church, blushing at the honor and the attention, stood ready to lift it up. "Sisters," she pronounced, "it's yesterday once more."

Some of the invitees gasped. Several more laughed out loud. Lying in state underneath the lid was what appeared to be a full-sized mummy. A cat dozed in its hollow rib cage.

"Karen Carpenter!" declared the spokeswoman.

Of course, it wasn't Karen; it was way too plump. But one club member was upset enough to call someone in from Christie's to prove that it was a fake before she defected to the American division. As the weeks went on, she was followed by almost all of the Karen Club founding members, as it became clear that a younger crowd—fashionable,

ironists—were taking over. For a while the Kentish Town
Kathedral became *the* hip London club to belong to. Female
celebrities groveled for membership. There was even talk of
admitting men.

But as lively as it was in London, the Tampa branch
was getting the most attention. American TV reported ma-
rauding bands of Karenistas roaming the streets, causing
terror among the unrighteous and abusing men. Blacked-out
male faces told the cameras in trembling voices how they
were captured and defiled, with Carpenters CDs (*The Col-
lection* being a particular favorite) playing some unnamed
part in their violation. Strident feminists would be given a
few seconds to explain to the camera that since history
began men have been making up stories of scary spinsters
ganging together to emasculate them and create social
havoc—usually getting cut off just as they started on about
witches and fires. Three women were later arrested—a de-
ceptively shy-looking vicar's wife who'd joined up when she
discovered her husband had been unfaithful, and two other
new members she'd persuaded to help her beat him and his
mistress up, remove their underwear, and wash them of their
sin. "It's what Karen would have wanted," they told the
police.

The Karen Clubs each issued its own official state-
ment. "The attempt by some misguided women to associate
Karen with either violence or soiled undergarments," said
the American one, "is an abhorrence. They have been ex-
pelled and an investigation is under way." Wrote Germany,
"We apologize unreservedly. We are reviewing our policy
toward unpopular groups." "It wasn't women," said the

Greeks, "it was gay men in Karen drag." Said Japan, "There's nothing wrong in traveling in groups. And you will know our members by their official Karen ID bracelets, on sale via our website." The British site posted the picture of a large pink heart with Karen and Richard, smiling beatifically, head to head, inside. It was underlined with the motto: "Sisters and Brothers Love One Another."

The official Carpenters fan club disowned them all.

Then something happened. Across the world, on the same day, at pretty much the exact same time, the paintwork on each of the Karen Club walls started to bubble. A dark excrescence collected at the bottom of the closed eyelids and moved up through the sockets, melting the paint as it went, leaving in its wake what looked like dark, piercing eyes. And a strange foam, some kind of fungus in the brickwork, started to appear between Karen's lips. It dribbled slowly out of her smiling mouth and along her chin, trailing down her breasts, right to the bottom of the wall and onto the pavement. When they saw it, some of the club members danced and rejoiced. Others fell to the ground and wept. Within moments, the leaders posted messages on their websites. By some miracle they were identical.

"By Her Holy Puke, Karen has declared herself sick of the deviancy of contemporary society and its music. Karen lives!"

The church of Karen was united.

I hadn't looked in on the Kentish Town Kathedral for a while. But last night, on my way home from the Underworld, I noticed that the place was in darkness. The curtains had been removed and the windows and doors were boarded up. There was a contractor's sign on the boards and a notice from Camden Council warning of dangerous falling masonry and telling us to keep away. Scaffolding buttressed the side wall. On closer examination, an occipital chunk had gone missing off the top of Karen's head. In the yolky lamplight, she looked like a napalmed hard-boiled egg. There were a few wet, scraggly bouquets kicked into one corner by the builders; some still had cards attached. I bent down and picked up a black-and-white photo of The Carpenters from which Richard had been carefully cut out. "We love you, Karen," someone had written on the back. "We want to be—close to you." I propped it against the wall and moved on.

# FROM A
# GREAT HEIGHT

Rex pissed off the balcony of the ninth floor of the five-star hotel onto the heads of two dozen fans. A news camera caught the whole episode. For several days on Argentina's national TV channel, Rex pissed over and over, pissed from several angles, sometimes in slow motion, with grainy close-ups of his open zip, his laughing face, and the fans down below. The newspapers went crazy. They called for the stiffest punishments: detention, deportation, *de-penisification.* The Archbishop led a service praying for his soul. A popular talk show host took a match to the band's record company promo photograph on prime-time television and told parents to do the same with their children's tickets to the show. Then they'd run the clip again: his smug face, his insolent decanting, and a fifteen-year-old girl, chief pissee, holding up to the balcony a drenched and happy face.

A tight-knit group of teenage girls had gathered, in tight tops and too much makeup, talking loudly, laughing, and tugging at their fishnet tights. Whenever someone clothed or coiffed rockishly appeared in the lobby, they'd squeeze out one of their number like a pimple, and she'd sidle over to the doorman and try unsuccessfully to chat him into letting her go inside to see if the band had come down. There were solemn boys in bandannas and cheap copies of the band's black concert T-shirts with the bright-colored comic book designs cracking off. They hovered separately, clutching magazine posters and records to be signed.

She'd been there, on her own, holding vigil since dawn. At three o'clock in the afternoon God smiled on her, Rex pissed on her, and the others gathered round her, reverential, jealous, touching the wet hair that stuck to her face.

When she came home the cat sniffed her, curious. In her bedroom she peeled off the piss-soaked shirt, held it to her face, then stored it safely in a plastic supermarket bag. Her hair was stiff and sticky and she pulled the longest strand into her mouth and sucked it. She stared at herself in the mirror. Her locket was piss-glued to the path between her small breasts. She took it off and laid it on her dresser and walked naked across the hallway to the bathroom. She had no desire to wash him off, but her mother would be home soon, her mother didn't understand, her mother believed the crap in the newspapers, her mother did not want her to go to the show. There had been reports of riots all along the tour; when the band refused to come back for an encore in Brazil, the fans erupted, they root-canaled metal chairs and hurled them at each other. In Mexico City cops cracked heads and fans dripped blood like statues of Jesus. The first night in Buenos Aires was sold out, over fifty thousand people, but they'd put on another show and she'd managed to get hold of a ticket. She was so determined to go that her mother would not have tried to stop her. If she hadn't seen Rex pissing on the news. On her daughter, on the television. Her daughter blissfully smiling as the man she's paid a fortune to see stands on the balcony of the *luxury hotel room* that *she* has helped to pay for, and laughs as he pisses down on her from a great height.

She didn't see the news program. She was in her bedroom, making up her face and fastening her locket when her mother burst in screaming and calling her names. She dropped the locket. It fell open on the dresser, and a driblet of golden liquid trickled out. Her mother left and locked her in her room.

She screamed and she cried, she prayed to God and to the magazine pictures of Rex that were taped above her bed. Her eyelids were puffed and quilted, her red mouth corrugated. She looked at herself in the mirror, and the pathetic picture she saw there made her cry even more. She beat on the door and called her mother all the filthy names she could think of. She made impossible promises to the Virgin Mary. But the door did not fly open, the walls did not tumble, night fell instead and she sat saggy on the bed, fat with tears, eyes swollen and fragile like eggs. She could hear the television in the living room, the happy babbling presenter, the insanely cheerful music. She wanted to switch on the light but would not give her mother the pleasure. Besides, she wanted to suffer more completely.

She heard her mother's footsteps walking to the kitchen, heard the fridge door open, knew from the snap of a ring-pull that she'd taken out a beer. She heard the footsteps coming toward her door, heard the key turn back in the lock, but still the girl did not move from the bed. She lay there like concrete, trying not to hear the TV in the next room, a singer crooning some yearny, clinging love song. She was swollen with love, raw with hatred, and utterly miserable.

She had no idea how long she had been lying on the bed; the darkness and the crying had jumbled everything up.

She felt feverish, wet and spongy. It was hard to see, but she thought she could make out people in her room. She recognized the doctor, their priest, her mother. Her mother was smiling, full of love and concern. She noticed she was lying on rubber sheets and that all around the bed there were troughs and the sound of running water.

She felt liquid flowing off her body. It was seeping up from under her cuticles, bubbling from the mosquito bite on her wrist, beading the palms of her hands and her forehead and her feet. It streamed from her locket and down the gutter between her breasts and over her small round stomach and into the troughs below. The doctor was taking her pulse, liquid welling around his thumb and forefinger as they circled her wrist, and smiling at her mother, and her mother was smiling back and scooping tiny glass bottles in the trough, and people were filing in and out of the room looking at her respectfully, just as they had looked at her outside the hotel. And they all want something from her—a cure, a benediction. A young couple stand hand in hand beside the bed wanting a blessing on their forthcoming marriage.

Then a clamor at the front door. Rex is standing in the doorway; photographers and news cameras wedge themselves behind him shouting questions and instructions to turn this way or that. His manager has his arms out, herding them off, smiling with his teeth, lying overtime, acknowledging their importance, promising them some undefined something special at some undefined later on. And he empties the bedroom, whispering conspiratorially to her mother as they go, "Should you wish to pursue a licensing deal for the product you propose to sell, Rex of course owns the rights to his own body products but I'm sure we could come to some arrangement acceptable to all parties."

And Rex stands beside her bed, his crotch just inches from her face, and drinks in her adoration.

Back at the hotel, the PR is fielding phone calls from newspapers and magazines all around the world. Dressed in her business skin, her face taut with efficiency, we overhear her saying, "As of this moment there is no talk of charges being filed against Rex. If it did come to a court case, his defense would be simple—preshow pressure and the responsibilities of performing to a hundred thousand people over two nights led to a temporary paralysis of the central nervous system and a consequent inability to control his bladder. I'm sorry? It's estimated at between three and three and a half ounces of urine voided. Hold on a minute." She puts her hand over the mouthpiece and asks the tour manager, who's just come into the room with the guitar player in tow, "What's three ounces metrically?"

The tour manager shrugs. "Fucked if I know."

"About a hundred milliliters," says the guitar player casually, and they both look at him shocked, as if he'd just discussed the Heisenberg Uncertainty Principle in depth.

The PR repeats the answer and hangs up the phone. It rings again immediately. Outside she can see a clutch of trembling teenage girls gazing up at the ninth-floor balcony. "Yes, it has been analyzed. No, there's no trace of illegal substances whatsoever. Just a moment." She picks up a notepad; the red message light on the phone is flashing its impatience. She reads with no emotion: "Water, inorganic salts, creatinine, ammonia, urea, and pigmented products of blood breakdown. You're welcome." A caller from the *New York Post* wants a comment on the rumor that urinalysis showed the singer to be HIV-positive and that the pissees' families planned to sue him for attempted murder. The PR sighs inaudibly, says something blandly quotable aimed at filling a column inch or two.

A call from Britain. A voice smarmy and familiar asks if Rex would like to take the opportunity to make a personal apology to his fans through the pages of the *Sun*. The PR's London office had faxed over the clippings from the British dailies an hour or so ago. A full page in the *Sun* showed Rex posed regally on the balcony, his eyes bright and steely with power and paranoia like the dictator of a small country, his hand just obscuring his open fly. The headline read: "WEE WEE'S BIG ADVENTURE," with "Rock's Bad Boys Say: Piss Off, Argies, Urine for It Now!" in bold type underneath.

Before she gets to answer that Rex isn't doing interviews, the guitarist grabs the phone and shouts down the receiver, "What's your problem? You want us to be *nice,* is that it? You want us to say sorry, we'll be good boys, we won't do it again? Rock bands aren't supposed to *be* fucking nice. That's not what we're here for. You go crazy if your politicians smoke dope or go to whorehouses, because that's not their fucking job. And it's not a rock band's job to behave like politicians and be polite and nice and try and please everybody all the time. Rock's *supposed* to be dangerous. These are dirty fucking times and we're a dirty fucking band." Grinning, he hangs up the phone and says to the publicist, "Who d'ya have to fuck to get a drink around here?"

The PR talks the manager into talking Rex into holding a press conference. At the huge oak door of the Presidential Suite the PR stands with a clipboard, checking off the names of the handful of handpicked journalists, making sure they sign the contract agreeing that the story will be published only in the X issue of X magazine and not be resold or syndicated. The journalists argue spiritedly about press freedom, while privately bristling about the future earnings they're going to lose as a result of not being able to sell the story to magazines that've been excluded for something unflattering they've written in the past. TV crews fiddle with their lights, plug their mikes into the PA system, and journalists hand back the signed papers and arrange their tape recorders on the table at the front. The band is already there, sitting in a row, but no one acknowledges them, everybody's looking at the door to see if Rex is going to show. He's late, as always, but they dare not start without him. Everybody waits and nobody complains.

And suddenly Rex is standing in the doorway, his bodyguard beside him, and all eyes turn. He's wearing tight black jeans and a cutoff white T-shirt with what looks like a road sign on it, a big red circle with a crucifix in the middle and a red line through it and the words "No Martyrs" written underneath. He's in the mood for talking, which is unusual. Words gush out of him and the journalists stoop to scoop them up.

"It's not *me* that's pissing on them, it's *authority* that's pissing on them. Have you *looked* at your fucking government lately, man? Or your police? Where were you and your TV cameras when the cops were beating the shit out of these same kids at the gig last night? You want to know what this band's message is? It's sticking in your face like a dick in a ten-dollar brothel and it's saying: *Question authority*, man. It's your *duty* to question the assholes in power. A fan's love is total. It is totally without limits. The *kids* aren't questioning what I did, it's the assholes in power that are giving me shit. You people have always gotten me wrong. I don't give a fuck what people say about me. Dirt sells; I'm not stupid, but there's enough *true* dirt out there, you know what I'm saying? You could at least get the stories right. I'm sick of being someone's fucking TV sitcom they think they can just switch on and off. I mean, how long was Jesus on the cross? He must have taken a piss, right? From a great height. Onto his disciples' heads. And did they crucify *him* for it?"

While he's soliloquizing, the band members ignore him. They sit either side of him and talk over the top of him like friends on a tube train separated by the raving madman who's got the middle seat. They laugh and mess with things on the table. The drummer picks up a little tape recorder, puts it on rewind, and holds it up to the microphone, and he plays back what Rex just said about Jesus while Rex continues talking with a five-second time delay, like on a phone-in program when the caller hasn't switched his radio off. The cassette recorder's owner looks a little desperate and tries to catch the PR's eye.

"Look, man, it's been twenty years since the Rolling Stones were arrested for pissing on a garage wall. Times have changed, the world's moved on. Don't you read your own newspapers? Jim Bayley left a fucking *turd* in the middle of his hotel bed and it wound up at Sotheby's, fetched a fucking fortune."

The journalists, like they always do, nod and laugh too loud. He continues at length, self-righteously, on the noble tradition of rock 'n' roll micturition, how The Who posed latrinally on an album cover, Ozzy made water on the Alamo, Izzy irrigated an airplane aisle—"Because," Rex says, pausing for emphasis, *"his fucking bladder was bursting,* and he'd paid ten trillion dollars to fly first fucking class, and when he needed to take a piss the toilets were all taken. *I* was dying to empty my bladder. The maid was in my bathroom. She'd been fucking around in there for over half an hour, probably going through my waste bin for used fucking condoms to sell to my fans. So what the fuck was I to do? I pissed out of the window. Was it *my* fault there were people out there staring up at me? Was it *my* fault a hotel that charges over two hundred and fifty fucking bucks a night can't spend some of it paying for security to keep them out of the fucking line of fire?"

A reporter from a South American daily dares to break into the monologue with a question. He stands up. All eyes turn to him. "In your song 'White Trash War' you caused a controversy in the United States with your attack on Hispanic immigrants. Is this incident merely another way of pissing on us?" Nobody has expected this; he looks so timid. Rex shoots up from his seat like an overwound spring, his eyes bright, his pale face livid. He knocks over microphones. He and his bodyguard are ready to fight.

The cat has jumped onto the girl's bed and is clawing the pillow. Circling, it lifts its tail and sprays on the wall behind. An oily yellow splash dribbles slowly down. She didn't know how long she'd been asleep. Or for that matter if she was still sleeping and only dreaming that she was looking at the clock and it was ten o' clock. There was still time for her to get to the concert. The band would go on late again tonight, she was sure. She didn't care what she had to do, she was going. If her mother tried to stop her she would kill her—a knife through the back of the neck while she was watching TV. Paco would take her. She would show him her breasts and he would drive her there.

And she stood at the top at the back of the stadium. From the distance the band onstage looked like fleas jumping on a white dog's back, but she could see Rex in close-up on the giant video screens on either side. Some people who recognized her from the television pointed her out to each other. A girl came up and touched her, two boys in new concert T-shirts still smelling of ink shuffled over shyly to talk. But she looked straight ahead at the screens. Hot tears puffed up in her eyes, and through them the image on the screen was squashed and livid like a rainbow melting.

# AND ALIEN TEARS

Jim's dead and Reeve isn't, which is why the Germans are here talking to Reeve and not to Jim. Though if Jim weren't dead, of course, there wouldn't be any need for them to be here at all. They're here to make a film about Jim, or more accurately, a film about the film about Jim, a TV documentary to tie in with the movie. They've rounded up the usual suspects—the director, the actor, the biographer, the record company, old girlfriends, rock critics who were rockcriticking back when Jim was still alive—but Reeve is their prize catch.

Reeve, so the story goes, was driving with his girlfriend, a Doors tape was on the stereo, and just as it got to their song "The End" the car swerved off the road. Reeve went through the windscreen. Three weeks in a coma and when he finally came to he told the doctor and his mother and his girlfriend and the clutch of faces peering down at him that he had broken through to the other side and he had seen Jim Morrison. Jim had supposedly told him to go back and that he would walk beside him, and the spirit of Jim had entered his body while he was lying blotto on the hospital bed. Reeve denies it now, says it was something his former manager made up to tell the press. "It's ridiculous. I never said that. That sort of thing doesn't happen to people. Dead guys don't just regurgitate into someone else." He calls his show a tribute, not an impersonation. "I like to think I help people remember what a huge talent he was."

Whatever it is, the shows are sellouts. Pale-faced young women with ironed hair and skinny grave-faced boys in floppy white shirts they bought in the girls department and leather pants with brass door knocker belts pile into the clubs and mouth all the words. Reeve's publicity blurb says: "The recession and the takeover of the music business by the big corporations have instilled a yearning for the honesty and simplicity of the sixties," which Reeve's Jim show is satisfying. Death is big business. Hendrix is alive and selling jeans, Elvis is flogging supermarket tabloids and fathering children up and down the country; if it ain't stiff it ain't worth a fuck. They flocked to The Doors film, and they flock to see Reeve with Jim walking beside him. The German TV crew was there last night, but there was a technical problem, and they've brought him back this afternoon to run through a couple of numbers again.

A nightclub by day unsettles you—too much light, not enough light, just enough to see the smell. Beer, old cocktails, stale cigarettes, ten years of accumulated earwax, most of the right nightclub smell ingredients, but they bear as much resemblance to a nightclub at night as the smell of airline food does to the stuff you eat at ground level. Daytime people smell different to nighttime people. Their movements are more spatial, their body-smells air-conditioned. Men in grubby band T-shirts strew wires across the stage; men in newer, cleaner band T-shirts strew wires across the floor. Two women walk around with clipboards, looking busy. Someone comes in off the street with sandwiches and coffee, and a wedge of dusty light beats him through the door, illuminating the shoddy tables, the tawdry decor, the black and purple badly painted paint. A nightclub has no right to be up at this time of day.

Reeve is upstairs changing. A rock journalist is being interviewed, they've clipped on a microphone, and he's sitting very still like you do when a movie camera is trained on you, not even blinking, like a rabbit caught in headlights. They look uncomfortable—the American journalist, the German interviewer—unsure of the dance steps, like a doctor going for a checkup or a cop arresting a cop. Should they act comradely? Antagonistic? Superior? Bored? Businesslike? The German goes for businesslike. "What were your impressions of Jim Morrison's sexuality?" and the American answers, "Well, it wasn't black rock 'n' roll sexuality and it wasn't white boys imitating black sexuality and it wasn't cowboy sexuality or New York greasers imitating Elvis imitating whatever. It was middle-class-white sexuality taken to its theoretic limit as the outer limit of your sexuality. What it was was the music of *your* dick." And you can see by the way the interviewer nods that he feels he's framed the question exactly right and has gotten exactly the answer he needed, exactly what he would have said himself if the positions were reversed. And they thank the American very much and give him a sandwich and a beer from the cooler box with the label slapped on sideways from sitting around in melted ice.

The band comes down, plugs in, tunes up. Reeve, in virgin pirate shirt and creaky leather trousers, goes over to the microphone and leans his forehead for a moment or two against the stand, his shirt flopped open, his arms crucifixional. He lifts off the microphone and encircles it with his dirigible lips, like he's sucking an ice cream, then holds it away from him and says, "Testestestestestest, one-two, one-two, one-two." The Germans make the international everything's-okay sign, and they nod in rhythm as a xeroxed "Roadhouse Blues" fills the fake night.

And several million Germans sitting in their living rooms see Reeve stalk the stage like a lion, his crotch shimmering in a leather-lizard sway. They see him pout the Jimpout, see him stare the Jimstare, the hooded one with the lids halfway down and the pupils halfway up, staring across the footlights, across the lines on the television screen and straight into their souls, while the music soars and swirls and curlicues about him.

And then they see him later, at home, being interviewed, and they gasp in amazement. Because the transformation is as total as werewolf back to boy. Offstage Reeve is small and skinny, slight and spare, fuzzy and vague like a bird that's fallen out of the nest. His eyes are small and birdlike. The only thing even vaguely reptilian about him is the bonelessness of his face. It's soft, almost chinless. They wonder, like you wonder when you watch a magic show, how he does it, how he makes those eyes, those chiseled cheekbones, the teen magazine picture-story-hero chin appear like that out of nowhere then disappear again. The only thing about him of any substance is his lips. He looks like a whoopee cushion impaled on a stick. And his eyes light up when he talks about Jim, and dim right down when he talks about himself. They screw up in concentration as if he were peering down a microscope into his life, trying to find something there he can recognize and label, and he scans his sentences desperately for a spot where he can slot Jim's name in again.

The TV station's switchboard is jammed with phone calls: thirty marriage proposals, two recording contracts, four death threats, and a book deal. A female psychiatrist calls to offer free advice. And all the next day's newspapers carry Reeve's picture, and the critics proclaim he's the star of the show. An East German poet, a famous former dissident, faxes in a poem he wrote while watching the show. In it Reeve becomes the symbol of a disunited Germany, the sad but cheery little East German who rattles about in the giant's leather jackboots and stumbles like Charlie Chaplin as he tries hard to keep up. He wants so much to emulate the powerful giant who always strides ahead of him, but he can only ever be a pale impersonation, an apologetic shadow, dickless, always the smaller of the two. When a lizard's tail is lopped off, it says in the last verse, the lizard keeps walking, it does not stop and look around to see its scrawny butt-end writhing in the dirt; it doesn't need it, it can do quite well without it, but the tail will go on wriggling behind it all the same.

*Die Zeit* calls up its stringer in L.A. to get an interview and runs it with the headline "The Lizard's Tail." It shows the pictures, the befores-and-afters, Reeve with his band and Reeve with his mum. He was fourteen years old, he says, when a schoolfriend turned him on to The Doors, lent him copies of *Strange Days* and *Waiting for the Sun*. It was like "a mystical experience. I went out and bought the albums and played them so often I played them literally to death. It was all I had of Jim. I never got to see him—he died when I was seven years old." He comes across as neither proud nor humble, but as a man who is comfortable with what he is. He merely takes for granted that people want to hear more about Jim Morrison than they want to hear about him, and it's a subject he knows an awful lot about. His answers veer among those of a first-year psychology student, a fan, and a science nerd.

"The Doors were signed to Elektra Records. It's a little-known fact that Elektra had the best-smelling album sleeves in the world; it was something in the ink they used. Jim was into smell. He had been heavily into the French decadents, and he once told the band that he wanted to smell Paris before he died. Did you know Jim was asthmatic? I don't know if it's true but I read it in an article written by his cousin. It was probably why Jim's father gave him such a hard time. His father was a military man, a rear admiral, and here he has a son who writes poetry and sniffs flowers, and to top it all keels over when he gets a faceful of pollen! His cousin said Jim's first experimentation with drugs was a deliberate overdose of asthma medication.

"If you want to understand Jim you first have to understand his relationship with his father. He hated his father and he hated the military and he hated the whole male domination and violence thing they stood for, and yet at the same time he wanted to *be* like that. He wanted to be the dominant male in a gang of men, he wanted to be the king of the jungle, and of course he wanted to dominate women. Totally. Also the name, Elektra—it was Electra who helped her brother kill their mother and her lover. Electra was like Jim's feminine half. You know those lines in 'The End': 'Mother, I want to . . .'? Think how significant it must have been for Jim to be offered a record deal by a company called Elektra."

The German TV people flew out to Los Angeles and offered Reeve his own weekly TV show. What the producers had in mind was a kind of Oprah Winfrey interviewing Michael Jackson, the difference being that their Oprah thought she *was* Michael. They settled for a cross between a European variety talk show with song-and-dance celebrities and an American freak show talk show, lots of weirdo guests espousing crazy theories while Reeve refereed.

They called it *The Lizard's Tail* and it was everything they hoped for. Everybody watched it, everybody wanted to be on it, from conspiracy theorists to rockstars passing through. From the teacher who was campaigning to have Jim Morrison's poems added to the school curriculum to the medium who claimed to have contacted Jim in heaven; there was a special heaven, she said, reserved for stars like Morrison, because the hordes still press to see them even when they're dead.

A German in his twenties who bore a slight resemblance to the singer came on the program and claimed to be Jim's son. His mother had gone to London to see The Doors in the sixties and as she stood crushed in front of the stage at the Roundhouse gazing up at Morrison, he stared back down at her, looking just like that photo that everybody knows, the lion picture, chest bare, arms extended, hair tousled, lips half parted, eyes staring straight into her underwear. And after the show she went to his hotel room. She married a publisher and became a Hamburg hausfrau and no one told him anything until a year or so ago when he argued with his father, who called him the bastard son of a fat L.A. rockstar poet, a drunk and bloated blubber Baudelaire who once had some talent but sold himself by the pound, and wound up wet and wrinkly, dead in his tub. And his mother became hysterical. She wouldn't cooperate when he went for the blood tests and applied to Jim's estate for the DNA. He'd changed his name by deed poll to James Andreas Morrison and his band was currently shopping for a major record deal.

An old rock musician, an old friend of Morrison's, who'd done acid with the singer "a thousand times" and had now joined the horde of cleaned-up campaigners, went on the show to proselytize. Reeve said, "I think the drugs thing was just because of his era; I don't think he would still be doing them if he were still alive. I'm not into drugs personally—my feeling is basically go suck a gun, it's quicker, you know?" And the audience applauded. "I don't even drink. Someone tossed a bottle onstage and I just stuck the bottle in my mouth, tilted my head back, and faked it. I stuck my tongue in the bottle neck so I won't take any down. I did do acid once, years ago, just to try and see where Jim was coming from. Only you can't really see what somebody else did, can you? I mean, it's a whole different thing."

A reptile keeper came on once with a tangle of limbs writhing in a box. It was a real lizard king, he said, five small brown lizards with their tails tied together, all desperately struggling to go their own direction but snapped back into the bundle like rubber bands. And he presented a lizard-skin belt once worn by Morrison to the teary winner of that week's Jimformation Quiz.

The East German poet came in and gave a recital. An Australian Doors copy band flew over for the show. Billy Idol, who was touring in Germany, came and sang "L.A.

Woman," which he'd covered on his album, and Reeve jumped up and joined him at the microphone. The next day's reviews said Billy's sultry Elvis-sneer looked like a cold sore beside Reeve's smoldering pout.

A music critic wrote: "What's refreshing about Reeve's performance is that there is none of the surliness, none of the done-it-all-before-to-the-point-where-I-hate-it-but-not-as-much-as-I-hate-*you* thing that you get from most rock artists you see on a stage. From Jim Morrison, certainly. The famous Miami '69 incident, the one where the singer was arrested for taking his cock out onstage, the one that is now cited as evidence of his coolness, his rebelliousness, his dedication to art, his *sexiness*? The truth of the matter was he was drunk. He had nothing but contempt for the audience, the show, the whole debacle. He couldn't be bothered. He forgot the words. He stumbled about.

"And when the people who had paid to come and hear him sing—and if he wanted to throw in a little of that famous wild-and-crazy behavior for the price of a ticket then fine, but the bottom line was they wanted to hear some *songs*—when they turned on him and for once the artist-audience hatred was mutual, he taunted them. He asked them, 'Do you want to see my cock?' And he pulled it out and it was *soft*. It wasn't cool or rebellious or artistic or sexy, it was soft and floppy as a dead fish.

"All rockstars at some point come face-to-face with the utter pointlessness of what they're doing. Some get there quicker than others, some hide it better than others, but it happens to all of them. Reeve, however, can never suffer from pointlessness. Because it's not *him*. The whole messy business of self has been done away with. He's doing it for someone else. He's been taken out of himself. He is like a religious devotee, he has that gleam in his eyes of someone who knows, whose conviction cannot be shaken, that there really *is* a point. In some way, Jim Morrison did die for him."

They did a special show on the third of July, the anniversary of Morrison's death. Reeve, dressed Morrison-esquely, tailed by the TV crew, walked around Paris, pointing out landmarks, places where Jim had or might have been. At the spot where Morrison died in the bathtub, the camera lingered on a mongrel dog pissing on the wall. Next stop, of course, was Père Lachaise cemetery, the camera moving sedately up the manicured aisle, following the arrows scratched onto monuments saying "Jim this way." It wove through tombstones splattered with graffiti: cartoon genitalia and declarations of love, snatches of Jim poems, often badly spelled, names and countries and messages in a dozen languages.

The graves were packed in tight like a ghetto. Jim's was hardly big enough to hold a circus dwarf. The stone was a squat plain slab the color of tarmac. It was mobbed with young people. They were sitting around talking and laughing, drinking beer and putting notes and flowers in the empties, placing them gently on his grave. It was really quite moving. Reeve melted in among them, kissed a few cheeks and shook lots of hands.

"I've made a lot of friends here," he told the camera. "It's amazing. It's like a sort of club. I've made the pilgrimage, I don't know, at least a dozen times. The first time I was eighteen years old. I brought a sleeping bag and camped out on his grave. The first time I came I wrote my name on his gravestone in the bottom right-hand corner. I wanted it to be right at '*The End*.' It's gone now. This stone is really ugly. The others got stolen piece by piece."

He led us up through the cemetery to where Oscar Wilde was buried. "Look at this." The camera closes up on the inscription. "The first time I came here I saw this. It's really incredible." He recited Wilde's words, etched onto the tomb.

> *And alien tears will fill for him*
> *Pity's long-broken urn*
> *For his mourners will be outcast men*
> *And outcasts always mourn.*

"It could have been written for Jim. 'Alien tears.' That's really something, isn't it?"

Cut to a bar where Jim used to come and drink and write poetry. The bar owner was rinsing out Pastis glasses, nonchalant and very French. A Parisian journalist in his late forties, who stated that he and Jim often had long conversations here about existentialism and claimed that Jim asked him to translate his poems into French, sat beside Reeve, perched self-consciously, arrogant and uncomfortable. He looked like he was sitting on a carrot and sucking on a lemon all at the same time.

And they showed footage of The Doors in concert and rare clips of Jim offstage, looking like a god and looking like a retard, Fat Jim, droopy-faced and bearded, with small eyes peering out of fat, puffy lids. And Reeve's band flew over to Germany and they played together for the first time in more than a year. And when they finished, Jim's cousin came out of the studio audience, shook Reeve's hand, and said, "Hello, Jim." There were tears in the audience's eyes, in the band's eyes. Reeve looked as if he were about to break down.

When the contract was up, Reeve chose not to renew it. On his thirtieth birthday he moved back to L.A. But his band had scattered and moved on. He went on a few chat shows, hired a media consultant, but nobody really wanted to know. He moved back in with his mother. He got a job with Star Company, driving a stretch limo, picking up VIPs at the airport. When the planes were late or his order was canceled, he'd drive down to the beach and sit in the car with the door open, letting the cool air in, writing poems in his head and staring at the sea. Feeling cold made him think about his apartment in Germany, the big old ornate radiator in the corner of the room, slow to rumble into action, reluctant to heat up the room. And the ceiling so high up that when he lay on the bed it made him feel like a child. He thought about the food shops, the cheeses and the sausages piled up in pyramids, a work of art, and sweets and cakes and pasta dripping in shop windows. He thought about the café that served poetic coffee in large silver pots with thick fresh cream.

And he thought about the German woman who had been his lover. She was older than him, almost old enough to be his mother. She was an artist, with strong hands and a strong, fine face. He had found her one night in the lobby of his apartment building, arguing with the concierge, who wouldn't let her up. He smuggled her in later, both of them feeling slightly ashamed and elated, laughing in whispers as if they were in his mother's house.

She told him—months later, when the concierge had come to know and accept her and would stop and have a natter with her every night in the hall and offer her a coffee if Reeve was late back from the studio—she told him what he already knew, that she was totally into Jim Morrison. She told him that she wanted to be on the show.

And she told him a story. She had gone to the cemetery at night and broken in, scaled the wall with a pickax and a spade. She said she needed to know for sure that Jim really was dead and buried. There had always been rumors, just like there had with Elvis, maybe just like for every star who dies in the bathroom, that he hadn't really died, that he'd just disappeared and was working in a gas station or living in a trailer in the desert watching the lizards go by. When reports reached Los Angeles that Jim had had a fatal heart attack in the bathtub, his manager had flown to Paris to see what was going on. And all Jim's wife could show him was a sealed coffin and a death certificate signed—she was so wasted—by she couldn't remember who.

If the coffin had been empty she had planned to go and look for him; she knew that she could find him. But it wasn't empty, she said, staring at the high ceiling as they lay propped up together on the oversized pillows. It was a while before he broke the silence and asked her what she did.

And he shuddered as he remembers how she tugged a cigarette from the packet and lit it, blew out a smoke ring he tried to catch. She said, "I gave him a blow job. And then I fell asleep." The cemetery caretaker found her the next morning. She was sent to a psychiatric institution. She still saw her caseworker; she wanted him to meet her. The caseworker approved of her going on the show. And it came to him that what he did was just another form of necrophilia, trying to suck some life out of a corpse, but he banished the thought as quickly as it had come to him, pulled the door closed, and started the motor up.

He drove up Sunset and parked outside the nightclub where the Germans had come to see him play. He watched the world hum by in its Porsches and Mercedes. He turned on the radio and waited for his ride.

# ALLERGIC TO KANSAS

Everything was fine until Leo started growing breasts.

Better than fine. Even Leo, with his well-honed sense of his own genius and matching grievance at how long it had taken others to catch on, viewed his achievements with some satisfaction, although he knew he deserved them and more. A number one album in Britain, a second one climbing the American charts, five hit singles, a sold-out U.S. tour, and a supermodel girlfriend who swallowed. And who had just called to say that her Caribbean shoot had been canceled and she was flying straight out to join him on the road. And who would be more than a little upset to see the teeth marks and lacerations that covered his torso, courtesy of the crazy blonde he'd shagged last night in Kansas.

"Tell her she can't come," said Murray. The tour manager knew all about the problems caused by visiting girlfriends. If he had his way, all females would be banned from the road.

Leo shook his head. "Ain't gonna work." No one said no to Phoebe Fitzwarren, and he wasn't suicidal enough to try. So he chose the grizzling option instead.

"Murray, she's going to be here tomorrow. What the motherfuck am I gonna do?"

Murray had experience in these matters. He'd worked with bands for years. Moments later he appeared with a huge roll of wide, crepe bandage, ordered Leo to strip, and proceeded to wind it tightly around his body, armpits to pelvis, pelvis to armpits, down, up, down. "Tell your old lady," he said, "that you tripped coming offstage and cracked a rib." And Phoebe had fallen for it—not just fallen, been smitten by such a fit of caring that she'd stuck around for almost a fortnight. Two weeks deep-frying under the stage lights like a burrito with legs—and no sex. Not even a hand job. "Broken ribs," Phoebe said, "can be dangerous. One false move, you could puncture a lung. Come on, baby, lie down here next to me, we'll just hold each other and talk." Which was just what he needed after two hours of staring down at rows of sweet young cleavage, feeling hornier than a Salvation Army band. He'd had to go behind Dave's drum kit for a wank during the guitar solo; he was sure he saw Ian's guitar tech laughing. He made a mental note to tell his manager to stop his end-of-tour bonus.

A hundred years later Phoebe's shoot was rescheduled. Finally he could take the bandage off. Her cab had barely pulled away when Leo shot back to his hotel room and ripped off his clothes. Standing naked in front of the mirror, he twisted an arm behind his back and tugged at the top of the wide strip of surgical tape that held the bandage down. It was stuck tight. He reached the other arm around, but it stayed put. Murray had done too good a job. Leo picked up the receiver and dialed. "The person in room 1–6–0–1," said a machine, "is not available. Leave a message after the tone or press zero for an operator."

"Murray. Where the motherfuck are you? Get your arse in here," he barked, and hung up. Impatient, he continued to worry at the bandage, grunting, swearing, trying to tug it around so that the tape was at the front and he could see what he was doing. It refused to budge.

"MOTHERFUCKER!" he bellowed. He picked his jeans up off the floor and dug in his pocket for the switchblade he always kept there. Flicking it open, he snagged the tip inside the top layer of bandage, carefully pulled it away, and sliced. The sharp blade zipped through the crepe, faster than he'd estimated, skidding to a halt on his pubic bone. A small cut but a deep one; it took almost a minute before the blood bubbled to the surface and started a slow drip onto his dick. "Motherfuck," said Leo, much more quietly than usual. One more inch to the right—the thought struck him dumb.

Hands shaking, he took a clean T-shirt from the top of his case and pressed it to the wound, lifting it up now and then to stare at the spots of red. Still trembling, he peeled off the torn layer of bandage which a fortnight of perspiration had glued to the rest. A loose end of bandage dangled at the bottom. "Thank the motherfucking Lord," he said, and started to unwind, round and around, carefully, as if his ribs really were broken, like his mum opening her Christmas presents because she wanted to reuse the wrapping paper.

After a while Leo's stomach appeared, its pale skin imprinted with the bandage's waffle marks. Next came his upper abdomen, white as an overexposed photograph. Only his chest left to go. As Leo tugged the last sweat-tight layer from under his armpits, two small, round, pert breasts popped out.

"Well, fuck me," said Murray as he let himself into the room, ready for any emergency, except this one. Two faces side by side gawped at the sight in the mirror.

"Jesus Christ, Leo." Murray gave a nervous laugh. "Like 'em so much you've grown your own?"

"Shut the motherfuck up!" wailed Leo, turning so fast from his reflection that he hit himself hard on the back of a chair. Which reopened the wound, sending the blood coursing a little more heartily down his thigh.

"Whew," said the tour manager, shaking his head. "I can see you're on the rag. I'd better keep out of your way."

As Murray left the room, Leo collapsed onto the chair. Only his breasts stayed perky.

When the tour manager returned, he was all efficiency. "Right, I've found a doctor, and he thinks it could be an allergic reaction to the bandage. You know, like some people get with a Band-Aid and their skin all puffs up?" In his short absence, Leo had crawled into bed and covered himself with the blankets; the swellings looked less obvious when he was lying down. His face peered up out of the sheets, glumly. "He'll be over within the hour to give you a shot."

"I ain't going onstage like this," sulked Leo. "You're gonna have to cancel tonight's show."

"Aw, come on," said Murray brightly. "The doc'll fix you up in no time. Think of it as a couple of big mosquito bites. They look worse to you than they really are."

The doctor arrived, examined Leo's chest, then turned him over and stuck a needle in his buttock. He wrote out a prescription for a course of antihistamines and antibiotics. "You're not to drink alcohol with these," he told Leo, and the singer nodded obediently. "Make sure he doesn't," he told Murray as if he were the patient's father, handing him the prescription, "or they won't work."

"I'll be back with these in a moment," said Murray, leaving with the doctor. Leo could hear them murmuring in the corridor. He sat up slowly in bed, checked his reflection in the mirror, hoping to see the mounds shrinking. They weren't.

"How the motherfuck am I meant to go out there like this?" Leo whined. He and Murray were backstage in the dressing room; the rest of The Nympholeptics were out sound-checking onstage. Leo's tight black T-shirt clung tightly to the small, round protrusions. "I see what you mean," said Murray, rubbing his chin. "Only one thing for it: We're going to have to bind 'em down."

"I'm not getting back in that motherfucking bandage." Leo shook his head and backed off. "I'm allergic, re-member?" Murray was already reaching for a roll of gaffer tape. "No, forget it," said Leo. "You're not taping me up with that." But he did. Taking it off wasn't pleasant; what few chest hairs Leo had went with it. If Leo ever needed a drink, this was the moment. As for sex, it was out of the question. While the rest of the band were getting drunk or laid, Leo went to bed alone, early, sober, and utterly depressed.

"Do you think they're going down?" Leo twisted his body sideways in front of the mirror. For four nights, the singer had been following the doctor's orders, to no avail. What could have just about passed as oddly overdeveloped pecs before had blossomed into a bosom any fifteen-year-old girl would have been proud to display. Murray shrugged and said he thought they were. Through the concrete walls of the backstage room, Leo could hear the band laughing at Ian the guitar player's impersonation of him as they sound-checked.

"I've been thinking," Leo said as Murray bound him up again—the gaffer tape had been replaced by a stiff, white cotton bandage; allergy-free, the tour manager had pointed out—"that it might have something to do with those two weeks I went without sex. You know, when Phoebs was there? I mean think about it, it can't be healthy for the body to just *stop* like that. You know, when you're gagging for it all that time and you can't get it?"

"Hmm," said Murray thoughtfully. After the non-stop fuckathon The Nympholeptics tour had been, he mused, the singer could have a point. "You mean it might be some sort of trapped testosterone? Kinda like trapped wind?"

"*I* don't know! But you try lying in bed with Phoebe Fitzwarren every motherfucking night for two weeks with a hard-on." The tour manager quickly swatted the agreeable image from his mind.

"Anyhow," Leo continued, "I figured that maybe I should start shagging again." Before Murray could point out the obvious publicity hazards he added, "With the bandage on, of course, and a shirt. Just try and undo this blockage, or whatever it is. Get my system moving again."

"Gotta be worth a go," said Murray solemnly, as if contemplating a risky operation. "I'll line 'em up for you after the show."

For the next week, Leo applied himself to the task assiduously. And although, as he resumed his alpha male role, band relations became smoother, Leo's chest didn't. Every night when Murray unwrapped him, behind locked doors when the concert was done, his breasts appeared plumper than ever. Leo returned to the path of abstinence.

"You know," the tour manager suggested when they reached New York, "maybe we should try leaving the bandage off? Could be all it needs is some air circulating around it."

"What! When I'm onstage?" shrieked Leo. "How the fuck is that supposed to look? Like the Britney mother-fucking Spears show?"

"I don't know." Murray shrugged. "I'm just trying to help. The doctors don't have any fucking idea what to do." Three more had been summoned, shaken their heads, and prescribed anti-inflammatories that didn't work. The pair sat in silence for a while, then someone was bashing at the door and rattling the handle. "Open up!" the guitarist yelled. "What the fuck are you two doing in there that you've got to lock yourself in?"

"We'll be out in a minute," Murray called back. Turning to Leo, he said, "You could wear one of those thick leather biker jackets. If you zip it up, no one will see a thing. Should be no problem picking one up in this town." The wardrobe girl was duly dispatched, and finally tracked one down in a cheap cutouts shop.

"What the fuck is that?" said Angus, the bass player, when Leo walked out wearing it that night. Angus was clad in the tiniest rag of a T-shirt; the arena was hot as hell. The crowd at the front were pressed in so tight they went home with their T-shirts steam-ironed.

"What's it to you?" snarled Leo. Angus threw a glance at Ian, who lifted his right hand from the guitar strings and made the "wanker" sign. It was not a great show. When it was over, Leo, lobster-faced and squelching with sweat, ran into the dressing room and bolted the door. Murray had to usher the band to an empty bunker at the end of the corridor.

"What the fuck is up with Leo?" Ian asked. His pants were around his ankles; a young woman's head bobbed in his lap.

"LSD," said Angus, unscrewing the cap from a whisky bottle. Lead Singer Disease.

"Can I have that when you're done?" said Kevin, the drummer. Angus held up the bottle. "No, that." Kevin nodded at the guitar player.

"I mean what's with that fucking jacket? It looks like shit."

Angus nodded. "He looks like a girl."

"It's like he's not even part of the band anymore," said Ian. The girl lifted her head, took a lipstick out of her purse, and put it on without looking in the mirror. Kevin gestured for her to come over. "I mean, all this shit with his own dressing room. Locked doors all the time. The only person he spends time with these days is Murray."

"Maybe he's turned queer," said Kevin, unzipping.

"The Judas Priest circa 19-fucking-80 jacket doesn't hurt your argument," said Angus, taking a long swig and burping.

"We should insist on a band meeting," said Ian. "Get everything out in the open."

Leo, his curves concealed by a thick, loose sweatshirt, unlocked the dressing room door and peered along the corridor. At one end two groupies in tight blue spandex, chained together, stared at him. Leo stared back, for a long time, but without lust. If he was looking at anything, it was for whatever part of himself could be found in them. He came up blank and turned toward the exit. Murray leaned out and beckoned them into the room.

"Hey, Murray, look at this!" shouted Leo. In the dressing room in Detroit, two days later, he'd found an old copy of the *National Enquirer,* and he was pointing at an article in it. It was a report on the increasing amount of female hormones in urban American water supplies. "Look. There was a study done in Kansas City—motherfucking *Kansas!* That's where *we* were! All these women taking the pill and pissing—that's it! I've been drinking female motherfucking piss-hormones!" Leo made a face and put down his bottle of mineral water.

"But you haven't been drinking tap water," said Murray, calmly.

"But the fucking caterers are cooking in it, washing the food in it. You should have insisted they use bottled water. If you'd been doing your job properly—"

It was against all the laws of nature for a tour manager to hit a star, but by Christ, did he feel tempted. "From what I've read," he muttered, "there are more hormones in American meat." By that night, Leo was a strict vegetarian—the reason Murray posited for the nagging stomach cramps that Leo had started to complain about.

Leo's breasts were blossoming on his new healthy diet. Since he'd stopped drinking, he'd slimmed down, so they looked even bigger. Leo thought his voice was becoming thinner too. 'That's it!" he announced as Murray appeared in his hotel room one night to put on the bandage—Leo had promised at the band's "openness" meeting not to lock them out of the dressing room anymore, but he had yet to mention the mammaries. "I've had it. I'm out of here," he said. Zipping the leather jacket over his naked chest, he picked up his suitcase—for the first time since he'd been on tour—and headed for the door. Murray blocked his path.

"Wait! MacFee's on his way over. He'll sort it out."

Clive MacFee, Leo's manager, was in Florida, where he'd been busy closing a deal on a substantial waterside property funded by his share of The Nympholeptics' hits. He was not happy at having to fly out to baby-talk his client, even if the plane ride wasn't exactly long; that was Murray's job. But the tour manager's calls had become increasingly agitated: MacFee's golden egg was sprouting ovaries. From what Murray said, Leo would be looking for work as a lap dancer if someone didn't do something quick.

"Leo wants to pull the tour," Murray had told him. "Impossible," MacFee had answered. "The promoters would sue the bollocks off of us—apart from which, the album's heading for number one in the States and I'm not having it fall back now. Call a fockin' doctor."

"I have. Three of them."

"Then call afockinother one. What do they say it is?"

"No one fucking knows."

In Leo's room, Murray's cell phone chirped. "It's MacFee. His plane has landed. He'll be here in twenty minutes. He's got a specialist with him," he repeated every line to Leo, who was trying to dodge past him, badly, like a girl playing football. "He'll take care of everything. He'll know what to do," he soothed, leading Leo back to the bed, helping him off with his jacket like a child.

MacFee blustered into the lobby, ignoring the concierge, still talking on his phone to Murray as he got into the crowded lift, the doctor three yards behind. The tour manager opened the door.

"Oh my good fockin' God," MacFee spluttered when he set eyes on his singer's B-cups. The doctor opened his bag and sat on the edge of the bed. The manager could not stop gawking.

"What the fuck am I going to do?" whimpered Leo. "I'm a worm, a cockroach. I'm a motherfucking freak."

"Don't talk like that," admonished MacFee. "You're a fockin' star. Top of the charts in the U.K. Thundering up the fockin' charts over here. Top five next week. Number one, I fockin' promise you, by the time you get to L.A." The last date on the U.S tour.

The doctor took out a hypodermic. "I've sedated him," he told Murray and MacFee as Leo dropped off to sleep like a baby. "He'll be out until morning. We need to calm his system down. He appears to be suffering an acute stress reaction."

"Ain't no one more fockin' stressed than me and *I'm* not sprouting tits," growled the manager.

"People react to stress in very different ways," said the doctor, patiently. "An imbalance in the endocrine glands is one of them."

"Can't you give him testosterone shots or something?"

"I think it will take more than that," said the doctor. "What he needs is to be isolated from all potential sources of tension."

"Well, right now," said MacFee, "he can't. "After Los Angeles he can have some time off—I'll book him in somewhere, get it dealt with. When the tour's finished he can do what the fock he wants—get a job as Madonna's fockin' body double for all I care at this present moment in time. Or have 'em off—there's always surgery. Thank fock there's no gig tonight." He looked over at Leo, sleeping peacefully. "I can rely on your cooperation," he addressed the doctor and Murray jointly, "and, it goes without saying, your discretion. Do whatever you have to do, but read my lips: The show stays on the road."

"In his present mental state, that might be difficult," said the doctor.

"Then we'll get him a fockin' shrink," barked MacFee. "A lot of bands have them on the road these days. Arrange one and send me the bill." He looked at his watch. "I'm out of here—meeting in Miami. You finished?" he asked the doctor as he strode out of the room. As he did so, a door down the corridor opened and Ian emerged.

"Clive," he said, "am I fucking glad to see you," and proceeded to list their grievances with the singer: They felt left out; he did things without consulting them; it didn't feel like a band anymore; something had to be done about the awful fucking jacket he'd taken to wearing—it made him look like a girl. Clive put his arm around the guitarist's shoulder, whispered all manner of flatteries and promises:

Leo was going through some changes, and it was important to bear with him; in two weeks' time the tour would be over, and there would be time off and big money; their album would be the U.S. number one. "Leo needs you fockin' guys more than he ever did," said MacFee, steering him back to his room. "You're a *band*. *Be* there for him. If you won't do it for him, do it for yourself. Do it for *me*. Ian, thank you. Without you there would *be* no band." The manager stiffened up, as if to hold back tears. Ian did too. "I'll see you in L.A. for the fockin' celebrations." MacFee smiled and gave him the high five. "Hey! Nympholeptics! Number one!"

Back in Florida, the manager was poring through a pile of press clippings, frowning. The latest live reviews were lamentable. "To drive the dictator General Noriega out of Panama," wrote one, "they played AC/DC at full volume. To prise the cult leader David Koresh out of Waco they played the sound of rabbits being slaughtered. If they want to flush Osama bin Laden out of the caves, they'd only have to broadcast videos of The Nympholeptics at the Premier Auditorium and he'd come crawling on his belly with his hands up. The band's frontman, who pranced about the stage like a drag artist, sweating heavily and constantly feeling himself up"—Leo had been scratching himself as unobtrusively as possible; the bandage made him itch—"sounded so much like a battered baby seal that you half expected a dancing band of Canadian fur trappers to come out onstage. A dancing band of Canadian fur trappers would certainly have had more charisma and star quality than this overrated, underachieving band."

The manager thumped out a phone number. Murray picked straight up. "What's going on out there?" Leo, Murray told him, was worse than ever. He had fired the shrink—said he didn't trust her. "Her eyes are too far apart—like sheep's eyes," he'd said.

"He had a problem with her fockin' *eyes*?" MacFee roared.

"We're not talking Jackie Onassis," said Murray, placidly, "we're talking close personal friends of her ears."

"But what the fock did she say was *wrong* with him?" MacFee thundered.

Her initial theory had been cocaine paranoia. A common problem with rockstars, she said. The bigger they got, the more their cocaine intake increased, which inflated their ego and sent it into battle with their id, the innate, unconscious feeling that they didn't deserve what they had and that it would be snatched away from them like a toy from a baby. Since, in order to become successful, artists suppressed these insecurities, she went on, they would either come to the surface as an obsession that someone or something was trying to stop them from doing as well as they could, or they themselves would do something, subliminally, to make their deepest fears come true. Get sick, for instance, or break a leg.

"But why the motherfuck would I grow tits?" Leo asked her.

"Unresolved issues with your mother," said the psychiatrist. "She tried to stop you becoming who you are, and those feelings are exacerbated by cocaine use."

"But she didn't try to stop me," Leo protested. "She was great."

"So great," the shrink went on, like a windup toy that hits a wall and simply bounces off in another direction, "you want to *be* her. You've produced a hit album, Leo, but that's nothing compared to what *she*, a *woman*, has produced. *You*. Whatever you've achieved, your unconscious knows came out of *her body*. The body that yours, Leo, is trying so hard to duplicate."

That night, when Ian and Angus went backstage to the catering area, they found Leo chasing the cooks, the wardrobe girl, even the on-tour gardener he'd had Murray hire to attend to his pots of fresh organic herbs, all in the direction of the exit ramp. "No more motherfucking women!" he was screaming. "Get 'em out of here!"

"What's going on?" said Angus.

"Leo wants all the chicks fired," said Kevin, who was sitting at an oilclothed folding table, pouring HP Sauce on a plate of sausages.

"Who's going to do the ironing then?" the bass player said.

"He says chicks are bad voodoo on the road," said Kevin.

"He just can't stand them," muttered Ian, "because they've got bigger tits than him." The guitar player stood close enough to them onstage to see them bouncing under Leo's thick leather jacket.

"Only just," said Angus. He'd seen them too. Their frontman, Angus and Ian had decided at their postshow

drinking sessions, was undergoing a sex change; he probably planned to get the snip in L.A. They were touring with
a trannie—which at least accounted for the mood swings.
Once Clive came by with their money at the end of the tour,
they planned to bail.

"I've found another shrink," Murray told MacFee
before the manager hung up. "A male one. Comes highly
recommended." He named some famous names.

Dr. Robert Mason was a big bear of a man: chest hair
sprouting out of his shirt collar, deep, stentorian voice. "Why
me?" had been Leo's first question to him.

"Did you ask yourself that when you became a
rockstar? Why me?" the doctor boomed back. "Because
you're *special*."

Leo took to him right away.

"Do you think I should have sex?" Leo asked him.
He felt he could talk to Bob.

"Do you want to have sex?" asked the shrink. "And
who do you want to have sex with? Your girlfriend?" Leo
shook his head. Phoebe was planning to meet him in Los
Angeles in a few days' time. He couldn't even bear thinking
about it.

"These 'groupies' you said you had sex with. Can you
tell me about them? How would you describe your sexual
relations?"

"You mean what do I do?" said Leo, and he couldn't
help smiling sentimentally as he recalled the countless com-
pliant girls he had commanded where to put what orifice and
what to do with it when it got there. The doctor listened,

unshocked, sometimes nodding sagely, grunting to himself academically at various descriptions of urination and cigarette burns.

"When you get big—as big as you are, Leo—you're like a supertanker that just keeps right on going. It takes no notice of what's going on around it, because it doesn't have to."

"I think I understand what you mean," said Leo.

"But in your case it's all happened so fast. Things can still get to you. It's growing pains, Leo, just growing pains. But back to sex—would you call yourself a breast man?"

"I would," Leo confessed. It was as good as a diagnosis.

"Next time"—the doctor closed his notebook and shuffled back his chair—"we'll talk about disassociation. You turn on the TV and you see yourself on the screen, or you'll open a magazine and the article you read is about you. You cease to live in your own body. It's a kind of public contamination. In our next session we'll figure out a way to decontaminate you."

After a week of twice-daily meetings with Bob, Leo was starting to feel pretty good about himself. When he went to bed at night and his breasts flattened out, he could dream they weren't there at all. The tour was nearly over, he could go home, his mum would look after him, it would all be all right. "You can look at it," Bob had said, "as an advanced form of homesickness. You've been away for so long that home has become an abstract. Before this, did you ever go on vacation with your buddies? Then you know what I mean when I say that a different set of rules apply. There's a different kind of normality. This tour is an extension of that."

Then, on the morning of the Bakersfield show, one month after the protrusions had first appeared, Leo was awakened by a deep, gnawing ache in his chest and a stabbing pain in his stomach.

"You are obsessing," Bob said when he complained about his bloated belly and tender breasts. "But it is not your fault, Leo. Being obsessional about your body is a by-product of your job."

"But it *hurts.* "Leo very nearly cried. He had been feeling tearful all day. He had a killer headache. "And Phoebs is coming tomorrow. And I've still got *these.*" He cupped his hand under his heavy mounds.

"What is the worst that could happen, Leo?" said the shrink. "I want you to think about that. Since fighting this thing hasn't helped, try the opposite. Go with it. And by the time you've discovered what is going on you might even have lost the urge to fight it. You never know—you might actually like it. Phoebe might like it too."

That night, just before the encore, Leo was doubled over by a fierce pain in his gut. He stumbled offstage into the dressing room, clutching his stomach, while the band stayed on, applauding the audience, in the hope of nurturing their enthusiasm to reciprocate. A halfhearted, slow hand-clap for more gathered pace around the arena. Leo sat on the toilet, in a cold sweat. The wound in his groin, which he thought had healed, had reopened, red and swollen.

There was blood trickling down his thighs. He rested his head against the cool tiled wall and wept.

The Nympholeptics' tour bus smelled of cigarettes, beer, empty Coke bottles, and men. The stickers on the windows read "I Brake for Blondes" and "Wanted: Meaningful Overnight Relationships." As it cruised down the freeway toward Los Angeles, Kevin dozed peacefully in his bunk, while Ian and Angus were watching *Fawlty Towers* videos for the umpteenth time. Leo was lying in the back, on the double mattress, stretched out on his side, his head in Murray's lap. Murray was smoothing his hair. The white bandage was now wrapped around his groin, stained with blood. Leo's pale face, never handsome, had become sweetly mournful. Transfigured somehow. To an outsider chancing upon them, it might have looked like they were reenacting Michelangelo's *Pieta*.

Sometimes in life something happens, a moment arises, an opportunity for if not complete understanding of what it's all about, then at least some kind of clarification. You're on one side of a line and you step into another. This may well have been one such moment.

Leo stared straight ahead and let it pass.

DIET COLA CANCER

Since you ask, yes, I did see her again, a couple of times as it happens. First time was back when Frankie Rose was still alive and organizing that Pussy tribute album. He invited me to drop by the studio to check out how it was coming along, and that's precisely what I was doing when Pussy walked in.

She had this strange way of moving—gliding almost, like a hot-air balloon cut off from its moorings. And one of the places she'd drifted, judging by the proprietary way she sidled up to him, was into Frankie's bed. All the while that the music played and Frankie scooted about on his chair, sliding the levels up and down on the mixing board and pointing out favorite parts, Pussy just sat there saying nothing, face blank, like she was contemplating something brain-numbingly dull but a darn sight more interesting than you or I could ever dream of being.

When it was over and I got up to go, someone announced that Pussy's car had arrived, which is how we wound up leaving together. She didn't say much as we negotiated the jumble of passages and fire doors and went out into a sour, London afternoon. If she remembered me from the interviews I'd done with her before her disappearance, she didn't let on. Then again, with the number of people stars encounter once or maybe twice in their lives, I guess every face they see must look vaguely familiar.

Her car wasn't there; the driver must have parked at the door on the other side of the building. There was just a bunch of teenage girls hanging out on the street. Most of them ignored Pussy—they were here for Frankie, although I suspect they were actually here for each other and Frankie was just the excuse—but Pussy didn't ignore them. She stood facing them, motionless, as if she wasn't quite sure what to make of this unusual audience. Then an older girl—eighteen, nineteen, who didn't look part of the clique—peeled herself off of the car she'd been leaning against and walked over to her. Pussy switched on that embarrassed, childlike smile she had whenever it looked like some kind of attention was coming her way.

The girl said something to her, I couldn't hear what. And all at once Pussy lashed out at her, arms whirling everywhere, all the while making this weird bellowing sound like a wounded animal. They must have been watching on the security monitors because seconds later two studio guys shot out and bustled the girl away. Frankie soon followed. He ran over to Pussy and held her by the shoulders—not intimately but quite formally, almost at arm's length, like they were a couple of awkward schoolkids being taught to ballroom-dance. The girls lined up in the curb like it was a mosh pit and stared at them both, grinning.

"What the fuck was that all about?" one of the guys asked me when Pussy had gone back inside with Frankie and the girls outside had been dispersed. I shrugged. His guess was as good as mine. Though I was to find out soon enough.

I was walking back to the tube station when a car pulled up and the back window rolled down. It was Pussy, offering me a lift. Since her flat was the other side of London to mine, it was curiosity more than anything else that made me accept. She clearly wanted to talk, although why she chose a rock journalist and not a shrink—other than the fact that we're definitely cheaper and usually better briefed—I couldn't tell you. I was surprised at quite how much she did say, though, considering how quiet she had been in the studio earlier, and considering her habit in the interviews we'd done before of doing little more than lip-sync the thoughts of the band's guitar player, her lover, Taylor, the man whose death brought on that weird disappearing act of hers.

"Do you believe in ghosts?" she asked me. She didn't wait for an answer. "I've been thinking about that a lot lately, whether there might be this invisible audience, you know, watching everything you do. Applauding sometimes. Sometimes chucking bottles of piss." She gave a small laugh. "Just, you know, *there*. So you're never actually alone."

"Is that how it feels," I asked her, "now you're back in the goldfish bowl?" and she massaged the frown between her eyebrows and stared out of the window at a woman trying to negotiate a baby stroller across the road between the moving cars.

"I'm not so sure it's a good idea," she said after a long pause. It was hard to say if she was referring to the mother and baby or her comeback. As our car turned the next corner into a quieter side street she remarked, "That woman at the studio. Do you know what she said?" For the first time since I'd got in the car with her, she looked me directly in the eyes, waiting for me to say something.

"No, but by the look of it, it wasn't particularly pleasant."

"She said Taylor had sent her to me."

"Hmm." I raised an eyebrow. "And?"

"She said that Taylor was watching me. That he knew everything I was doing."

"Him and Jesus Christ," I muttered.

"And she also said she was fucking him."

"Taylor, not Jesus, I take it?"

She frowned.

"Look," I added, "one thing I do know is that weirdos will never worry about extinction. There's always some nut giving Jim Morrison head or having Elvis's love child. It's the celebrity-death thing. They can't get their brain around it. They're crazy about someone they never knew in the first place, so the lack of the little green blip on the monitor isn't going to be of any great significance to them."

"No," she interrupted, "it wasn't like that. She said she didn't care whether or not anyone believed her because soon enough we would know the truth. Because *I* wasn't the only one who was making a comeback, she said—*Taylor* was too."

"I'd say you were in a better position."

"No listen, she told me Taylor had laughed at the idea of me trying to do a record without him. She said he told her to tell me, 'Anyone can make a start in rock music. It's the end that kills you.' And it just sounded so much like something Taylor *would* say that I flipped out. I think if they hadn't stopped me, I might have killed her."

As she spoke, her face was blank, like someone utterly defeated. If it hadn't been for the fact that half an hour ago I'd seen what was going on between her and one of Britain's hottest young popstars, I'd have said that this was a woman who still wasn't over the shock that when Taylor died, she didn't die too, since all her energy had been wired up to him. When we pulled up at her place, she shook my hand distractedly and said good-bye, like at the end of an interview. I noticed that she was wearing a silver identity bracelet with the name "Taylor" on her wrist. "Let's meet again sometime," she said. She didn't invite me in.

Do you remember when the story broke in the tabloids about Pussy and Frankie Rose? Early one morning a postman had seen them slipping into Frankie's houseboat— sorry, "love boat"—and he figured the newspapers ought to share in his joy. After several nights stalking them, the paparazzi were rewarded with a front-page shot of the couple's faces, smudged with sex, framed by the boat's small wooden doorway. The *Sun* did itself proud:

> Mad for the Buoy! It was **old** hands on deck when the 25-year-old pop superstar invited the 41-year-old former rock singer Pussy on board his **Love Boat** to show her his captain's log! Since Frankie first moored the brightly painted canal-boat the *Bloody Rose* outside his swank, £3 million home in London's exclusive Little Venice, there has been no shortage of beautiful girls lining up to scrub his plank. Which makes his latest choice in ship's mate even stranger. Pussy—real name Terri Allen—is **old enough to be his mother!** Nevertheless the odd couple gave the local fish a few headaches as they rocked and rolled the boat all night long! When we asked Frankie about the new woman in his life, his answer was unprintable. As for Pussy, she's saying nothing—mum's the word!

A sixteen-year age difference, and from the fuss the papers made you'd have thought she was a pedophile. The rock press wasn't much better. One of them said she should change her name from Pussy to Snatch, as in "cradle snatch." Little wonder she and Frankie kept the relationship quiet. Odd thing, though, is that even when they were all over the papers, they never really went public. Not even when the rumors appeared that she was pregnant with his child.

She was in Los Angeles with Jack Mackie, her manager, to sign a big American comeback deal—Frankie planned to produce her album—when she flicked through the channels on her hotel television and stopped on MTV. It was a news report—shaky video footage of her lover dying on the pavement outside a North London nightclub in another woman's arms. Pussy didn't scream. Didn't even cry. She just quietly left her hotel room, walked the few yards up the hill onto Sunset Boulevard, and lay down in the road. Just lay there. If it was a suicide attempt it was a pretty bizarre one— the cars, inching along the boulevard at their usual funereal pace, had no trouble stopping, in fact were so used to grinding to a halt for no reason that no one even hooted. Then Jack came running up, held up one hand like a cop to stop the traffic—which was already motionless, but I guess he felt the need to do something useful—and scooped her into his arms.

Holding her close to his chest, he carried her down the hill and along the covered, fairy-lighted path that led into the Eden West lobby. The staff were lined up and watching, as if the master was returning with his new bride, carrying her over the threshold. Someone held open the door to the pool and Jack swept through, past the gawping guests sitting by their low-calorie snacks at the poolside café tables, past the power-swimmers and maids and the Mexican gardener hosing down the giant leaves of the tropical plants in the hotel's back garden, and carried her into her suite, laid her down gently on the bed, closed the blackout blinds, and crept into the next room to phone the front desk and tell them that under no circumstances should they be disturbed.

The story I heard was that after Jack left her room, Pussy emptied out the minibar and stared at the TV until the news report came back on. That night she started bleeding on the carpet. When the maid found her the next morning, curled up on the floor in the center of the stain, she refused to leave for the hospital until they'd cut out the blood-soaked patch of carpet and put it in a plastic laundry bag in the empty minibar. It might have been apocryphal, of course— there had been a number of those kind of stories doing the rounds since Pussy had gone public about her breakdown and told how for years she'd obsessively hoarded all her hair and body waste and everything, I don't know, either afraid of letting go of the past or reclaiming her body for herself.

All I *do* know is that the record company booked her into the Shining Star Institute—the rehab-cum-psycho spa that Cal West's controversial shrink had set up for rich, damaged stars. I was interviewing one of its regulars, Carrie Gibbs, not long afterwards, and she told me she was there at the same time as Pussy and had tried to befriend—as she put it—"a sister in need." But Pussy wouldn't speak. "Not even in psychodrama class," said Carrie, which she found most unsettling. Carrie had had her septum rebuilt four times, had been arrested once for stalking a former boyfriend after he quit their band, and still wouldn't gig in any town with an h in its name on the advice of her psychic, but the concept of a star who didn't want to talk about herself was about the sickest thing she could imagine.

But, coincidentally or otherwise, Shining Star was exactly what Pussy needed. When she finally left the place, it was arm in arm with, of all people, Spike. He'd just spent three months in the Institute's sex addiction clinic—part of a deal his lawyer managed to broker with a California judge who loved his records, after one of Spike's less salubrious encounters with a young fan. Judging by the smile on Spike's face, the regime wasn't quite as harsh as the U.S. court system might have liked.

Despite the fact that Pussy was over twice the age of Spike's usual choice of companion, the relationship continued in the outside world. I'd never have believed it, but Spike did wonders for her. The big test was the night he took her to the Whisky a Go Go to see Kunt, that Pussy tribute band; she passed with flying colors. Spike and Pussy held hands at the back of the room, swinging their arms back and forth like a couple of besotted teenagers, as three girls in boy-drag and a guy up front in peroxide wig, fishnets, and fuck-me shoes ran through all her old hits. Spike laughed uproariously when Pussy's doppelganger opened the drawers of the filing cabinet on the left of the stage and bombarded the whooping crowd with jam-dipped tampons, More surprisingly, Pussy laughed too. No one had ever seen her so animated. By all accounts they were inseparable. Until, that is, that night at J.D.'s.

J.D.'s Bar & Grill was the hottest nightclub on the Strip. Its owners were three big-name actors with delusions of rock stardom who had a side band by the name of Meat. Because of their work commitments, Meat didn't get to play too often—for which music lovers can offer up thanks—but when they did, *real* rock stars, enticed by the kinds of girls and drugs serious film money could buy, would always come by to hang out or jam. Which was how it was on the night of the Diet Cola Incident.

Just after midnight, after a set by a forgettable local band, Meat took the stage, to exaggerated cheers. Each time it launched into a cover song, someone in the room would urge a celebrated tablemate to get up and join in. Pussy had insisted, despite Spike's objections, on a table at the back, out of the range of fire, but the actor-bass player spotted her. "Pussy!" he yelled, pointing her out to the lighting man, who followed his arm and put a spot on her. The actor-drummer tattooed out a drumroll that sounded like bean cans tumbling downstairs as the bassist jumped off the stage and slalomed between the tables to where she was sitting. He bowed to her flamboyantly and, asking Spike's permission, took her hand and pulled her up out of her chair. As she let him lead her to the stage, the audience stood and applauded vigorously, like at the Oscars. Meat fell to their knees and salaamed in extravagant worship. It was the first time Pussy had set foot onstage since Taylor's death.

The band struck up the old Pussy hit "Sleepwalker." For a moment no one, herself included, was sure if she would sing or run away. Then she lifted the mike off the stand, her eyes preternaturally bright. She crossed her right leg over her left and swayed on the spot like a little girl. She fingered the microphone provocatively and gazed across the heads of the celebrity crowd. At Spike. Who was gazing at the pumped-up breasts of the teenage blonde who'd taken over Pussy's chair and was assiduously, meticulously massaging the cock jutting from his open fly.

Pussy sprung off the stage. She landed awkwardly on one foot, breaking a stiletto heel. It gave her a lopsided walk as she lumbered through the staring faces back to where she'd been sitting. Spike was grinning. The girl's mouth was frozen into a startled sex-doll O. With the agility of a center-forward, Pussy aimed her foot at Spike's crotch. Her shoe, already fatally damaged, flew off and hit the signed, framed black-and-white on the back wall of Johnny Depp playing a guitar. Spike laughed uproariously and raised his glass to her. Pussy shimmered with rage.

Her eyes zoned in on the bottle of Diet Coke the girl had been drinking. So perfectly, so ludicrously Californian. No alcohol—the girl was under twenty-one—and God help her if she lit a cigarette, but hand job, no problem. Snatching up the coke bottle, Pussy hurled the contents over them. The way the girl screamed, you'd have thought it was boiling oil. She kept on screaming until the lights came on and all eyes, those of the actor-band in particular, were on her. The waitresses came by with clean towels, wiped the chair, replaced her drink, led her, soothingly, to the ladies' room. The next day, Pussy moved out of Spike's Franco-Beverly Hills château and into a suite overlooking the back gardens at the Eden West hotel.

Which is where she was the next time I saw her. I'd been summoned to Los Angeles by Rex, the singer with the heavy metal band Shoot 2 Kill. A perverse character, he had announced that he was going to make a solo album with a middle-aged country singer, LeeAnn Starmountain. Since for some reason I'd not yet quite worked out Rex had adopted me as his private Boswell, he told his record company to fly me to L.A. so he could discuss the project with me. I'd have done a lot more than that at that particular moment for a flight out of London—a long story, maybe I'll tell you later—but I stood my ground and insisted on a room at the Eden West, and that's what I got.

As soon as I checked in I changed into a bikini, grabbed the plastic bagful of British magazines and Sunday newspapers I'd brought for the trip, and headed for the outside Jacuzzi in the garden at the back. The Jacuzzi was empty, steaming in the evening air, a sunken circle tiled in black, dotted with tiny underwater lights and framed by a mini-jungle of glossy tropical plants. A world smelling of jasmine and chlorine. There was a wooden post with an intercom and a big red button that connected to the front desk. I pressed it and ordered a large, crushed margarita. The Jacuzzi sprang into action and I stepped into the bubbles forcing their way up through the water. Leaning back, I rested my head on the tiled surround. Hot water pummeled my shoulders, a cool breeze skimmed my face.

The waiter soon appeared with an enormous stemmed bowl of gray-green slush. He placed the tray by the pool, took out his lighter, and touched it to the tequila in the scooped-out lime shell on top. It twitched into flame. I signed the tab damply and peeled the *News of the World* off the top of the pile. On the cover of the newspaper was a pneumatic young blonde who looked all of sixteen, and a smaller inset picture of Spike. Big red letters told me to turn to the center pages for the full story, and I did as instructed, sipping my margarita. When someone spoke my name the glass almost flew out of my hand.

It was Pussy. She was standing on the edge of the steps dressed in a fifties swimsuit and a white hotel bathrobe. "Hey there, mind if I join you?" She dropped the robe carelessly by the steps so that the bottom dangled in the water and stepped down and sat right across from me, stretching herself out, her feet floating up through a carpet of froth. The bubbles coughed at her bathrobe, willing the rest of it to fall in.

"What are *you* doing here?" she said with a smile, like she'd run into an old friend. "When did you get in?"

"Just arrived, twenty minutes ago," I said, and outlined my mission. When I got to the subject of Rex, her eyes lit up.

"That guy has the *cutest* butt, don't you think? But I hear he's pretty psycho."

I confirmed that both observations were true. Pussy shrugged. "Hey, all the men in this town are either fruits or nuts. A girl needs a dick transplant to get laid around here." I didn't think it would help this unexpected new atmosphere of fellowship to point out that until a month or two ago she had been dating Spike and that she didn't look as if she'd been too deprived in that department since.

"Mmm," she said, eyeing my glass, "good idea." She reached out and hit the red button. I noticed that the Taylor identity bracelet was gone. "Drink up," she commanded, "there's another one on its way. So, what's the gossip back

home? Ah!" she said, spotting my pile of publications. "Are
those new? Brilliant. Can I?"

"Help yourself," I said, instantly regretting my gen-
erosity when she went straight for the *News of the World*. I
didn't think she'd find the cover story as entertaining as I
did. But I was wrong. Pussy devoured the tale of Spike's
affair with the young girl she'd thrown the glass of Coke at
with complete delight. She shrieked at certain passages and
read her favorite bits aloud.

"Did you see this?" She put on a dumb Valley Girl
accent and read, "'I am not what you would call a shrinking
violet, but when Spike first stood before me naked I was
alarmed! I had never seen anything like it. He was enormous!
Hung like a horse.' *A horse*? What was the poor child on? The
man needed tweezers to jerk off. Oh, hello—" The waiter had
just arrived with our drinks. She looked up at him sideways,
through her eyelashes—the old Princess Diana trick; men
can't resist it. You could see the effect it had on the waiter.
"Be a sweetheart, would you, and put these on my account?
I'll take care of you later."

For over an hour we sat there and talked. Every now
and then my brain would do a double take, wondering if this
could be the same two-dimensional poster girl I'd interviewed all those years back, or the lost soul in the back of
that car in London. Whatever that Shining Star bunch had
done to her, Pussy certainly seemed changed. She was vi-
brant. A real talker, and a champion gossip—people told her
things, and she had no qualms about passing them on. There
was one story she had about—I'd better not say his name—
a top ten singer who paid young boys to crap on glass-topped

coffee tables while he lay with his head underneath. The kid lost his balance, the glass broke, the star got a mouthful of shit and splinters and was hospitalized, as Pussy nicely put it, with "chronic coprophilia." The only reason I'm telling you this is to show that bodily functions did appear to still hold a fascination for her, whether or not all that stuff about her lost years in New York was true.

There was something she said about Spike too that stuck in my mind. "Some people are born with the rockstar gene. Me, I never ever considered myself a rockstar, but Spike definitely did." When I asked her what, in her opinion, a "rockstar" was she said, "Rockstars live in a world that kind of looks like the real world the rest of us inhabit, but it's more like one of those parallel universes they had in the old sci-fi comics, where things look the same but have completely different functions. They have these huge houses they don't live in, because they're always on the road. They have fancy cars they don't drive because they've always lost their license. They have wives they don't make love with, friends who hate them, families who resent them, magazines they don't read except to see if they're in there. You know," she added, "it was always very, very difficult for Taylor."

"Why?" I said. "It never appeared to me that he was finding things hard—quite the opposite."

"It was hard because Taylor wrote all these brilliant songs, but he'd written them for a woman to sing—see, that's really where the problems came in. Because he needed a woman who would sing them exactly the way that he would—but of course any woman who could do that wouldn't have been a woman, if you get my drift."

"So he figured he could go to some rock 'n' roll IKEA and pick up a flat-pack of the perfect woman and just bang it together?" I said.

"Kinda," she said. "He used to go to this cocktail bar where I worked. And he used to sit at the table and just look at me. But not like the other guys there looked at me—more like observing. I said to him once it looked like he was planning to paint my picture, and he said yes, he was doing something like that. That I was his Dream of Art and Beauty Made Flesh." She said it like each word was capitalized. "Other guys, it would have bothered me. I can't explain, but with Taylor it didn't. We became good friends. And when he put the band together—in the beginning it was this big joke that we were all in on and the rest of you weren't; we would laugh about the Pussy calendars and Pussy condoms—we'd sit around, Taylor, Johnnie, Robbie, Chas, and me, coming up with the craziest merchandising ideas. Pussy credit cards where you'd earn Pussy miles that got you free entry to lap-dancing clubs if you were a guy. I can't remember what we figured the girls would get.

"I guess I didn't realize at the time that Taylor wasn't really laughing. As far as he was concerned, he was Pussy. At the end of the day, what it really came down to was he wanted to be *me*."

"Ach," I said—the drink must have gone to my head, since I don't normally do bad impressions of German psychiatrists in company. "Vat ve haff hier is a classic case of vagina envy."

"You know," she said, laughing, "you could be right." Then the smile disappeared. "But what can I say? I adored him." We both stared at the bubbles for a bit. Pussy broke the silence. "I've been reading this book on Andy Warhol, Taylor's favorite artist. There was something he said that stuck with me: When your personal philosophy runs out, you have to tread water for a bit because you just get fed up with being *you*. I can relate to that, I really can. But," she said, brightening, "maybe it'll be easier this time around. Because this time *I've* chosen it."

I could hear voices. Two gay guys—an Englishman in a sarong, an American in a tiny black swimsuit and two big hotel towels over his arm—were heading toward us, bickering. "May we join you, ladies?" the American asked as he shimmied into the water. The Englishman lingered on the edge. Ignoring us, the American continued his quarrel.

"Oh do get real, honey, if *you* had her money and you looked like that, *you* wouldn't do something? Even if you didn't have the money!" He sank beneath the water and surfaced in a waterspout of bubbles. The Englishman rolled his eyes as he lowered himself in. "If I was Streisand I would Not Change a Thing."

Pussy tossed back the last inch of her margarita. I could sense our time was up. "Well, time to make a move," she said. As she got up out of the water the Englishman put his hand over his mouth and screamed, "Pussy! Oh my God, oh my God, I don't believe it. I am your biggest fan."

"Thank you." Pussy smiled her honeyed smile, and the man melted. His companion looked unimpressed. "Well," she said, using me as an excuse, "you must be shattered; go get some sleep. See you tomorrow?" Aware of our eyes on her, she sashayed slowly up the steps, curtsied to pick up her bathrobe, hung it over one shoulder, and walked to her apartment like a star.

The Englishman was beaming. "I do not believe that I was in a Jacuzzi with Pussy; pinch me!"

"She has *not* aged well," muttered the American. "Did you see those thighs? That's not cellulite, it's a cry for help." I gave him a withering look as I stepped over his legs and out onto dry land, but he probably couldn't see it in the dark.

I didn't see Pussy the next night, nor the one after that—Rex pretty much monopolized my time. The third night, my last, I went to the Jacuzzi but Pussy wasn't around. After that it was back into an economy window seat and heading for home.

After a wait at the Heathrow luggage carousel that was almost as long as the flight, I wheeled my case unmolested through customs and stopped to buy a newspaper to read on the tube. It was a cold, gray morning, still making its mind up if it could be bothered to rain or not, and I was too tired and dispirited for anything more than a desultory look at the pictures; whatever they were they'd be an improvement on dingy suburbs and a Tupperware sky. Then, as the train disappeared underground, I noticed Pussy's picture in the Showbiz section. It said she was being sued by the hand-job girl. "Diet cola," the news item quoted the lawyer, "is known to contain potential carcinogens," and his young client—currently undergoing cancer counseling and trauma therapy—was demanding five million dollars for medical endangerment and emotional distress.

What was it the Ghost of Taylor said? Anyone can make a start in rock music, it's the end that kills you. Another bundle of gray-faced women in black Puffa jackets and men in cheap navy suits surged unsmiling into the already-packed carriage. As they pressed into the narrow gap between the seats, the newspaper was pushed into my face. The words and pictures blurred into a Rorschach stain which bumped and vibrated before my eyes as the train continued its long lurch east.

# I KISSED WILLIE NELSON'S NIPPLE

"My grandma taught me how to fish, play poker, and find myself a husband. My other grandma taught me how to save my soul. Grandma One had six hundred record albums, all of them country music. She used to say, 'Country music is life. If you love life, you'll love country music.' I despised country music. When she died she left me all her records. I took 'em down to the used record store, traded 'em in for some rhythm and blues records and an old saxophone. Never did learn to play it—my mother wouldn't allow it— but I tell you, girl, with that old sax I learned to give the best blow jobs."

LeeAnn Starmountain clasps my arm with her red-taloned nails and smiles a big, wide, lacquered-lipped, country music star smile.

"Then a friend called me up one day and said, 'My husband's left me.' Around about that time I was having trouble with my man too." A bluebottle circling our bar table lands in a puddle of spilled red wine and spins around, around, buzzing, on its belly. Without missing a beat, LeeAnn picks up the magazine I brought along for her to see where our interview will wind up and rolls it tight, lowers the tip toward the swimming fly, and—slowly, so as not to make a mess—scrunches it into bluebottle paté.

"So we drove to the bar and got us something to drink. We drank all night. When we walked out of that place we couldn't even stand. It was the worst weather in forty years and the snow was up to here. And there's this old guy lying on his back in the snow—dead, drunk, I don't know; maybe he's just fallen over. So I say to my friend, 'I'm gonna go check on the old guy,' and I go shlooping back over to where he is—I made up that word, 'shlooping'—and I say to him, 'Hey, mister, d'ya need help?' And my friend is laughing fit to piss her pants. And I say, 'What?' And then I see it, and I *scream*. He's got his thing out, and he's pumping away at it in the snow with his eyes closed—wonder it didn't snap off in the cold. 'Go on,' my friend says, 'help the man.' And we're both laughing and trying to run at the same time and getting nowhere, it was like sleepwalking.

"Whenever I get seriously drunk I sleep three hours exactly and then I'm bolt upright, wide awake, and there's nothing can get me back to sleep again. So I got up and went down to the kitchen and made some coffee. And I started thinking about that old guy back there and how he was dealing with all the shit life had thrown at him far better than any of us were. And that's when I started writing country songs."

She's a handsome woman—in her late forties, though she looks older. Mostly it's what she's wearing—everything too tight or too bright, too low- or too high-cut. That and the ozone-eating hairdo and trawled-on makeup that make her look like your mother trying to look sexy. If it weren't for the American accent, she'd be right at home behind the bar of this down-at-heel London pub chosen simply for its proximity to the arena where she's playing tonight. Funnily enough, four days ago I was in a different drab London pub, this time interviewing her ex-husband—her fifth if you're counting, "Big" Willie Bean. It was just after last weekend's Royal Command Performance, when LeeAnn opened the show with a cover of the Queen Mum's favorite, "Stand By Your Man." "Big" Willie was in the audience, and when LeeAnn hit the chorus all six-foot-four of him stood up and shouted, "Which one, you cheating bitch?" and they gently but firmly led him out. He told me later, "My ex-wife put the cunt into country."

LeeAnn was the oldest of seven girls. Judging by the photos they all looked like their mother, who looked like Tammy Bakker, all hairspray and thick black mascara and Jesus. Or, in LeeAnn's case, two out of three. Her mother loved God, and LeeAnn hated her mother. She married her first husband on her sixteenth birthday to get away.

"Tommy Moorhead was the cutest guy. Moorhead by name, Moorhead by nature. I was fourteen years old when we first did it. My mother would have killed me. The bad thing about having sex so young is you've got nothing to look forward to later. The *good* thing about having sex so young is it's *bad*. "She laughs out loud. "I was fourteen and Tommy Moorhead was eighteen and he could say 'I love you' in more ways than a Barry White record. One night we were out walking in the woods and he stops and unzips and takes it out and asks me to touch it. Begs. Gets on his knees in the mud and the leaves and, tears in his eyes, *pleads* with me." I'm suddenly aware that all this time, unconsciously, she has been running her middle finger and thumb up and down the tightly rolled magazine. Seeing me look at her hands, she misunderstands and says, laughing, "Oh I didn't have these nails back then, honey!

"Well, I could never stand to see a man cry, so— you're not going to print this, are you? The worst thing is I've always had a real strong sense of smell, and Tommy's thing smelled warm and damp, ammonia-y, kinda like a dishwashing cloth. Then, when he put the rubber on, it smelled more like dishwashing gloves. In the end I guess it was all so domesticated-smelling I figured I might as well marry him. It lasted, God help me, five years."

He was a lineman for the county. He drank and he beat her, then he cried in his beer. He played around. Her dog died. Class-A, straight-down-the-line country material. She packed her bags and went back to her mother, and her mother prayed and beat her some more and sent her back to him again.

"Like I said, that's when I started writing country music, which I'd do of a night when my husband was out working, or whoring. Days, I waitressed in the diner. One day somebody left a magazine behind. There was an article in it about California and sunshine, and I was sick to death of the cold, so I was like, Right, where do I buy the ticket? I hocked my saxophone and I was outta there. It was tough in the beginning, sure it was—L.A.'s a hard town, looks soft on the outside, but inside it's as hard as steel. I saw an advertisement in a magazine that said, 'Unusual extras wanted for film work,' and since I didn't look too much like the other folk in Los Angeles I figured maybe this was my break. Turns out they were looking for hunchbacks and Siamese twins.

"But their office was right next to this big bar in Encino, name of Cactus Joe's. Maybe you've heard of it? It got real famous; all the big country stars performed there.

And they were the first bar in California to install a mechanical bull, way before that whole big *Urban Cowboy* thing started happening. Come on, you've never seen a mechanical bull? You haven't lived, honey!" The way LeeAnn explains it, it's like a tailor's dummy you'd use if you needed to make a suit for a bison, that's stuck on pistons that jerk it about. You get on, and you try to stay on, and if you're a man and you turn the timer to ten and the grader to eleven you can banish any further thought of fatherhood.

"Though there was none of that back when I first went to Cactus Joe's. It was an old-fashioned, spit-on-the-floor, drink-two-bottles-and-piss-five kind of cowboy bar. But they had a job going, and a job is all I needed. I slept with the guy who ran the joint to make sure I got it, too, and then I wound up marrying him. Shit, I don't know, girl, I guess I'm just a serial wife."

Cactus Joe's was the first place Mrs. Wayne B. Marvin ever sang her songs in. Mr. Marvin wasn't too hot on the idea at first, but his customers seemed to like it, and before long it was making him money and the place was getting a reputation. Dolly Parton put in a surprise appearance when she was playing in town and got up and sang with LeeAnn. After that, all sorts of musicians would show up. LeeAnn sang with them all.

"The thing about Los Angeles—which is something you would never even dream about back home—is you're meeting people all the time, and when you're not meeting people you're meeting *people's* people, and then all of a sudden someone's saying, 'I'm gonna put you together with so-and-so,' or they write down a number and say, 'Give so-and-so a call and use my name.' Which is how I ended up in a recording studio with a hotshot producer, making my first record. I don't have the happiest memories of the experience. Wayne B. wasn't exactly being the supportive husband, you know what I'm saying? I'd come home from the studio, four A.M., excited as a kid, and what would I get?" She jams her lips together. "The silent treatment. Maybe a grunt if his team had won. Have you ever felt like a severed leg, honey? Because that's how it feels lying there all night, hot and prickly, adrenaline running, staring at the back of your man's head." I nod—sincerely, as it happens, making a mental note to deal with the unresolved issue that was sitting up smoking a cigarette in my bed when I left home an hour and a half ago.

"Then Lee Starmountain came back into my life—the very same day, as it happens, that my third album went to number one in the country music charts. I hadn't seen Lee Starmountain—yes, Starmountain is my real name, my married name, the third one, he got my money and I kept his name—not since I left home and came out to L.A. I was crazy for him once, big-time, but seeing as how he was a friend of my husband's—my first husband, Tommy Moorhead, who didn't even need an excuse to give me a beating—and since he was also pretty tight with Doreen Swensen, who was more than a little psycho and would have taken my baby blues out with a nail file if she'd seen how I looked at him, I left him well alone. A smart move, since he told me Doreen did do some unofficial eye surgery on some other girl after I left town—which is why, when we met up again, Lee Starmountain was a single man and Doreen Swensen was in the crazy house, dribbling down her nightdress.

"Things had gone from bad to worse with Wayne B. I had no one to turn to, I was tired and worn out from the tour, it was hotter than hell, and I was feeling kind of homesick—I don't know, for the cold, for real life maybe. It's easy when you're at the top to forget that the bottom's full of shit, and you just start wanting to wallow in it again. I was in the limo coming back from the show when we drove past a truck stop. Lee Starmountain's truck was in the parking lot. I'd know that truck anywhere—a huge red semi with a charred chrome muffler sticking up at the front, and mud flaps with chrome cutouts of nude girls, and the bumper sticker, 'My Truck Is Like My Woman: Touch Her and You're Dead.' I told my driver to drop me off.

"We slept in the truck that night with the radio playing and I swear, it was the most exciting night of my life. Better than being onstage and ten thousand people applauding. Better than the Grammy. Better than meeting the Queen of England. I know what they say about country men, but I'd rather have a man breathe tobacco on me than mouthwash. I like to smell a man sweat—shows he's a man. I'd had it with those music-business men who smell like they've had the fumigators in, and when you have sex the sperm come out with their hands up and little gas masks on. Anyhow, one thing led to another with Lee, and we got engaged and we got married, and then we got divorced. Why did we break up? Well, it's all in my hit song, honey: 'He Wore Out His Wedding Ring on the Steering Wheel.' Lee was always off in his truck somewhere, and not always alone. And I've never been the kind of gal to chew my nails and wait for my man to come home."

She married husband number four on the rebound. Another Wayne—E. Wayne Woolf, a tour promoter who promoted himself to her manager, robbed her blind, and beat her soundly. Her clippings file had pictures of LeeAnn and E. Wayne in the tabloids, huge dark glasses not quite covering her swollen cheeks and eyes. Then one night, driving home from the bar, E. Wayne spotted the license plate on the car in front of him. It read: '911 NOW.' Which E. Wayne took as a sign from Jesus that it was an emergency. That from this moment on he should give up drinking and music and all other godless things (though he negotiated an exclusion on the beatings) and follow the True Path of the Lord. When he came home, sober, clutching a Bible, LeeAnn left him. "I don't remember all the violence," she tells me. "Just the greatest hits."

By this time she'd recorded eight platinum albums. She'd won two Grammys and several CMA awards. *People* magazine put her on its cover. A writer and photographer went to her hometown to interview her family and her mother shouted at them through the screen door that her daughter was a whore. They had a picture of Tommy Moorhead, who was no longer the cutest guy—he'd lost most of his hair and some of his teeth and a beer gut was poking through his checkered shirt. His sentiments on his childhood sweetheart pretty much echoed those of his former mother-in-law. Wayne B. could not be interviewed, since he'd been shot dead in the Cactus Joe's parking lot by a crazy drunk last year, but the magazine ran that wedding photo too, *and* the one with E.Wayne, and a picture of Lee and LeeAnn, standing by a semitruck hung with streamers and silver horseshoes and white flowers, smiling like two kids in love.

"When Lee and I fell apart, it hit me like never before. Or since. I drank too much—I know I fucked too much, anyone who would buy me a drink. Not that I couldn't have afforded to buy my own—for Christ's sake, I bought a fucking bar, I bought Cactus Joe's and gave it to Wayne B., God rest his soul, to get him off my back—it's just, we don't do anything without a reward really, do we? A drink, a cigarette, even just a hug. It was not a good time for me at all; I was kind of drowning. E. Wayne Woolf *Enterprises*"—she scraped quote marks in the air with four scary red talons—"wasn't much of a life belt. Really it was getting that part in the Willie Nelson film that pulled me through.

"Yeah, that was the film where I got to kiss his nipple. I kissed Willie Nelson's nipple. That was weird. But Willie was a great guy, he really stuck up for me—I was giving everyone a hard time, turned up late on the set a coupla times, with the drinking and all. I didn't really know that I wanted to kiss Willie Nelson's nipple, but that film sure turned me around. What did it taste like? Hell, girl, you're crazy! I guess I didn't do it too well, because that was the first and last film part I got offered."

"Excuse me?" A young man with a North London accent and an utterly nondescript appearance has come over and is hovering at a safe distance. LeeAnn looks up and gives him a radiant smile. He just goes on standing there; he doesn't appear to actually want to say anything else. She holds out her hand and says, "Hi, I'm LeeAnn." "I know," he says self-consciously. "I just wanted to say I'm a big fan of yours and, er, well, that's it, actually, I just . . ." "Well, thank you," says LeeAnn graciously. "Which is your favorite record?" The guy looks pinned to the spot. He says, like he's afraid to say it, "Well, actually, *Two's Country*, the album you did with your—" He stops short before the word "husband" and substitutes, "'Big' Willie Bean."

"Well, that's one of my favorite records as well," says LeeAnn, beaming. "Thank you—what's your name? Gram? Oh, *Gra-ham*. Thank you, Graham. It was a pleasure meeting you." Poor Graham looks like he's going to dissolve on the spot. He turns to go, remembers something, and thrusts a beer mat in front of her, then grunts something inaudible which LeeAnn, bless her, interprets correctly as an autograph request.

"Willie Nelson," she says when we're alone again, "was the one who introduced me to Willie Bean. Like I said before, I figured one Willie was as good as another and a 'Big' one better still, but"—she grabs my forearm again—"don't believe all you read, honey. Men *lie*. But Willie Bean came into my life right when I needed him. He'd been a hard-living man, a country singer of the old school, and he'd had problems with drinking and drugging of his own. He was cleaned up when I met him, and he cleaned me up too.

"It was kinda weird being with Willie Bean at first. Up to now I'd been the big star in my relationships, and I was getting kind of used to it, though it came with its own heartaches—men don't like you to do better than they do, it eats away at them and they can't get it up no more, and of course that's your fault. But with Willie Bean and me, we used to take it in turns. I'd go sit in the wings when he did a show and watch the crowd go crazy for him, and he'd sit in the wings at my shows and do the same for me, and the audience would see him and they'd make me bring him out and sing with me, and he'd drag me out onstage to sing with him as well. And then we figured, Hell, we might as well just do our shows together, so that's what we did.

"He was a wonderful man, Willie Bean—a Capricorn, and Capricorns are real romantics. Never laid a hand on me. He was never mad at anyone, not as I know of; I guess I was the first. He used to say to me, 'Women are such beautiful creatures. You can never figure out the way they think. I think that's why God put them here on earth, to make us men think all the time so we'd have something to do and stay out of trouble.' I guess in the end there were three things wrong with Willie Bean. He believed in God, he believed in me, and he wanted to stay out of trouble. I guess I should have met him while he was still a hard-living man."

There's another young man standing at the table, even younger than the last one, maybe all of seventeen, but this one doesn't look shy at all, and he's gorgeous. A tall, thin, leather toothpick of a guy with an enormous blue-black quiff. He bends over; at first I think his neck and shoulders can't stand the weight of his hair, but he's bending down to kiss LeeAnn on the lips. "Can I get you something, darlin?" he drawls in a Southern accent. He has cheekbones you could shave your legs on, except he would have to shave mine first. Everyone in the pub is looking at his hairdo except me; I'm looking at the enormous stiffie straining to break out of his leather pants barely six inches from my face. I can't take my eyes off it. LeeAnn must have noticed; she grabs his butt.

"Meet Joe-Bob," she says. "A couple more beers would be nice, angel." "Sure thing," he says, adding, "Nice to meet you," although she hadn't told him my name.

"Joe-Bob," says LeeAnn while he's at the bar, "is my guitar player. Seventeen years old." I guessed right then. "I'm taking him on the road with me—I'm not letting this one out of my sight! Anyhow, you want to have something for the girls to look at as well, don't you? You can't work with older guys because as they get older they'll have either made it as a musician and have their own thing going, or they won't have made it and so they hate you. And old guys always have encumbrances—families, house payments. I think women are so much more flexible, we can work out those little problems much more easily, but I don't like playing with other women on the road, they're too goddamn competitive. So that only leaves younger guys. Tough, huh?" She laughs. Joe-Bob returns with our beers, runs his hand along LeeAnn's cheek, and goes back and sits at the bar.

Does Joe-Bob make her feel like a kid again? I ask, pretty stupidly, but it's hard to think of anything smart to say when all your blood has abandoned your brain and gone to your genitals.

"Hell no!" she exclaims. "Being a kid again—I dreamed about that not long ago, being back home in my bedroom with my sisters and my mom and dad in the next room. I woke up scared stupid. It's number one in my top ten of things that scare me stupid, followed by waking up in bed with my first, my second, my fourth, and my fifth ex-husbands—I still have a soft spot for Lee Starmountain—then waking up and finding I'm waitressing, or finding out there's really a God, or losing my mind, or losing my teeth, or my tits, or anything beginning with T until you're up to ten."

She hadn't been back home again since her mother died.

"Shit, that was one crazy time." She gives a skewy laugh, but you can tell it wasn't funny. "My mother. It was January—real cold. My father had been real ill and my sister—the youngest one, who lives in San Diego; they all moved far away as possible eventually—she told my mother she was coming over to take my father back with her for the winter. Which caused a mighty row, my mother figuring on Southern California as the next best thing to Sodom. But my sister, good as her word, flies out and fetches my father, who is too gaga to protest even if he wanted to.

"Like I said, it was a bitter winter. So cold that my mother got up in the middle of the night, stood on a chair, and took down the suitcase off the top of the wardrobe where she'd packed away their old electric underblanket the year before. She pulled off the bedclothes and strapped it onto the mattress, plugged it in, turned it on, and remade the bed and lay down. The effort made her ill and she reached over for her pills and they say that's when she had the stroke. Couldn't move—couldn't get her pills and couldn't turn off the blanket, which was a real old one, no thermostat, just kept getting hotter and hotter. And she broiled on it for a whole week before a neighbor thought to call the cops.

"I didn't really accept that she was dead till I saw her laid out in the Chapel of Rest. It was my mother all right, looking like one of her overcooked Sunday roasts. My sisters all kissed her and cried, but I couldn't do either. I took a taxi to the airport and flew right on out of there and when I got home I went to the nearest bar and said, 'Take everything you've got off those shelves and pour it into one big fucking glass.'"

Her new manager comes over—one of those sharp-suited-young-businessman types, nothing to do with country but fingers in all sorts of pies. Though not LeeAnn's, judging by the way he's looking at Joe-Bob's behind. I figure he must have heard where the conversation was going.

"How are you two doing?" he asks solicitously, which all journalists recognize as shorthand for "Time's up, interview's over, now fuck off." The pub's starting to fill up anyway and people are staring at us. Show time's less than an hour away.

"Lord, is that the time?" says Lee Ann exaggeratedly. "I do go on. I hope you have everything you need." Joe-Bob comes over and gives her his arm and helps her up like a real Southern gentleman, and there it is again, at eye level. A hot ball of lust grips my crotch and glides up my insides like a Lava lamp. I think I'm falling in love.

"Have you ever been in love?" LeeAnn asks me, and I must have blushed because she pats my arm and says, "You don't have to answer, honey, I was just being curious. Just wondered how it would be to ask *you* a question instead. You know, you're the first woman interviewer I've had in a long time. Usually I get men. We girls have to stick together. A lot of women say they can really relate to my songs. They say, 'This is my song,' and I say, 'Yes, honey, it is.' The best songs are like listening in on a private conversation, don't you think so? Well, it was a real pleasure talking to you— I'm sorry, what was your name again?"

# SPITTING IMAGE (THE '80S RETRO TRACK)

Perry Kaye was number one. Princess Diana loved him. Quite how much she loved him led to a good deal of speculation in the press. His lips were ripe and full without being meaty or dangerous, his chin was lightly stubbled, and his hair, short and wavy, was slicked back off his face. He had a part in a bad soap opera and a worse Lloyd Webber musical and an album and two singles high in the charts. He had just released the second part of his autobiography, *Don't Just Sit There* (*It's Your Life, Get On With It*); part one, *You Can Do It* (*If You Really Want*), still topped the *Times* best-seller list. His face was in all the Sunday magazines, and his butt was in tiny cycling shorts. Whatever you thought of Perry, his ass was a masterpiece. What Elvis was to lip curls, Perry was to butts. So when Spitting Image made Perry's puppet they started at the bottom.

The original plan was to recycle the puppet of Andrew Ridgely of Wham!, which had been sitting in a cupboard since the first series, but no one could find it; it'd probably gone the same way as Andrew Ridgely. Then someone came in from the storeroom waving Samantha Fox's talking mammaries. And in a studio that smelled of scorching latex and looked like the Texas Chainsaw Massacre— dripping heads and limbs on meat hooks above vats of steaming glob—they prised off Samantha Fox's puppet's lip-nipples and messed with the electronics so that each buttock rolled and bumped independently. And from piles of photographs they built the perfect popstar parody. Not an easy job when most popstars are already parodies of themselves.

Not every famous person loved their Spitting Image but Perry did, with its fat red lips like double-parked London buses, how when they parted in a smile the other puppets would throw their arms across their eyes to shield them from the dazzle. He loved the sketch where his puppet sat at a desk chewing on a pencil, scrawling titles with lots of brackets in and scribbling them out, while Princess Di, gooey-eyed, hovered by him with a Biro, playing join-the-dots with the stubble on his cheeks. He adored the "Botty Ford Clinic" sketch, where a puppet George Michael, shamefaced and in shapeless trousers, shuffled into a room full of aging popstars whose rear ends all spread over the edge of their seats. As each of them got onstage to confess their backside backsliding, Perry's puppet watched from the corner, his tight round buttocks sliding gaily from side to side like a cow chewing the cud.

He sat in front of the TV with his remote control and reran the videos over and over. He decided without bias that his was the best puppet Spitting Image had ever made. He had to have it.

Clive MacFee, Perry's manager, called the TV company. First he tried to get it for nothing, in exchange for promises of lots of valuable coverage in the press. They laughed and said it wasn't for sale. Finally, after long negotiations, everyone agreed on a sum that equaled the economy of a small third-world country, and Perry started readying his home for its arrival.

The den—the room where he kept his gold and platinum records and framed photos of himself with his arm
draped chummily round Donald Trump, Madonna, Michael
Jackson, Fergie, the Pope, politicians left, right, center, and
Cicciolina, and Princesses Diana and Stephanie, plus the
statue of him currently on display in the Whitney that Jeff
Koons had made—would henceforth be Puppet Perry's
room. Decorators redid the white walls and matte-black
designer minimalism in Saudi Moderne rococo red and gold.
Heavy gilt frames now encased the awards and pictures. Fat
rugs squatted on the floor. In the center of the room stood
an ornate French daybed. Perry's personal assistant was
kneeling in the corner, blowing up the sex doll that Perry had
sent him out to buy, in a moment of inspiration, as a partner
for his puppet. He propped it up on the pillow, where it sat
staring dumbly, its red mouth yawning, its plastic pussy
puckering between splayed pointy legs.

Perry decided he should throw his Spitting Image
a "Welcome Home" party. MacFee called up columnists
and all his famous friends. Paparazzi scaled his walls when
word got out that Princess Di would be there, and hurled
abuse at an army of shed-shaped men in dinner jackets who
threatened them with castration if they didn't remove
themselves pronto to the other side of the street. Flashes
flashed as Mick and Jerry, tailed by Saint Bob and Paula,
glided up the pathway and through the door. A famous
politician sat on the daybed swigging Cristal, while two
even more famous footballers kicked the blowup doll across
the floor. Perry wove among them, theatrically cuddling,
noisily kissing everybody's lips, gripping their shoulders

and jumping back dramatically to ooh and aah at their svelte-ness or their clothes. He accepted their outsized compliments with a burr of his eyelashes and a birdlike wiggle of his butt. He chatted with the selected journalists and posed beaming with designers, stars, and supermodels for the photographer his PR had hired for the night.

Then one of the footballers—purple-faced with alco-hol, bouncing the sex doll up and down on his knee and tell-ing no one in particular, since everyone had moved away from him, that Perry's puppet's condoms should be made of human skin—suddenly ejaculated: "Well, where is it then?" And the whole room, as it does, went suddenly silent. They looked at him and he grinned sheepishly and repeated, more quietly this time, "Where's the bleeding puppet?" And Perry's smile imperceptibly melted and a droplet of cold panic dribbled down his spine. His manager felt it across the room and teleported to his side.

By means of ancient codes and ventriloquism, Perry, while continuing to smile and chat, communicated to the man paid to take the cares of the world from his shoulders so he could devote himself to art that the limo with the pup-pet was due two hours ago and he was not a happy star. And that if any of his famous guests should leave before it got here, heads would roll—as heads do, starting at the top.

Which is when one of the dinner-jacketed gorillas appeared unexpectedly. He was clutching a large brown Jiffy envelope, ostentatiously wrapped in a bright red ribbon. He explained that it had been tossed from a passing car. Every-one looked; the manager stepped forward to take charge. He maneuvered the security man into a back room. He took the padded envelope and held it up to the light uselessly, rattled it like a birthday present, stood staring at it as if it would tell them what was inside of its own free will. He squeezed and prodded the padding, looking for wires. He asked the security guard for his knife. He carefully prised up one of the staples, sweating. He peered in the hole; he couldn't see anything. He sniffed—it smelled of rubber. He worried some more staples out.

Inside was a Polaroid of Perry's puppet. It looked like a wounded soldier from the Crimean War, with a red-stained bandage wrapped around one side of its head. There was something quite heavy in the bottom of the envelope. The manager turned it upside down and it fell onto his hand. It was a rubber ear with red paint crusted on it. And a note made out of letters cut from *Smash Hits* magazine. MacFee was reading it as the *Sun*'s gossip columnist came nosing around the door. He saw the bloody ear, screamed, and dropped his glass. The manager walked over and slapped the lump of rubber into his trembling hand. "Perry's puppet," he said, "has been kidnapped." And their faces lit up as if someone had turned on a switch behind their eyeballs with glorious visions of headline marching upon headline, of column inch marching upon column inch.

Three daily tabloids put the kidnapping on their cover. Perry loved publicity. He had two full-time publicists on his payroll and a clippings service that sent him a package almost daily. He still had the first thing ever written about him cut out and yellowing and folded in his wallet so that if one day he should lose his memory or the world should forget him he could take it out and unfold who he was. He loved publicity, but he loved the puppet more. Really loved it, like popstars loved their model wives, like Michael Jackson loved Bubbles.

He couldn't work, he couldn't sleep. And when he did he had fitful charcoal dreams filled with images of captivity and torture, of people and things he'd half heard about when MacFee made him go on that Amnesty tour. He'd wake up feeling like a worm had been chewing him inside out. He'd reach for the telephone, then put it down again; there really wasn't anyone he could call. Just columnists, rival popstars, and people on his payroll, and any one of them could have done it, if he stopped to think about it; the bastards all hated him enough. He tried recalling a time when he still had friends, people to hang out with. He thought about his first band, Swallow. They'd done everything together. Until he dumped them for a solo career.

He picked up the phone again and hit the top button and bawled out his manager, who bawled out the publicist for telling the press, as they'd told her to, just how much of a fortune Puppet Perry had cost. He fretted that all the coverage would feed the kidnappers' egos, make them take their time, keep raising the price. They didn't say in the ransom note how much they wanted, just that they would send instructions, and if he failed to pay they'd send the puppet back to him piece by piece.

Ten days went by. Perry was nervous as a spider, up early each morning for the first time since his school days to check the post, call the office, see if anything had arrived. There were tearstained letters of condolence from teenage girls on mauve writing paper, a couple of encouraging faxes from fellow popstars' management offices, the expected weirdo stuff, like the letter telling him to look for it in Princess Diana's apartment in Kensington Palace, and the package with the joke-shop rubber penis tattooed with his name.

And then it came. His assistant, looking terrified, crept in carrying a white Chinese take-away box. From the way he held it it might have contained cat-sick. On a bed of noodles sat two rubber fingers like fat spring rolls. And a photo of the puppet propped outside a restaurant in London's Chinatown. Its two remaining fingers were raised in a rude sign at the camera, its now-unbandaged one-eared face looking puzzled and forlorn. The assistant shook his head: There wasn't any letter. Perry cried out—it had been building up; he couldn't stop himself—"It's not fair!" He could feel the tears welling in the back of his eyes as he picked up the fingers and rolled them gently in his hand. "They said they'd tell me what to do and they didn't! It's not fair!"

The audiences who flocked to the Lloyd Webber musical had to be content with Perry's understudy. Perry, lied his manager, was extremely sorry to have to let his fans down but he had been smitten with a bad case of the Asian flu. The soap opera writers had to rewrite furiously, sending Perry's character to Florida to search for his missing granny, who had cashed in her pension and run off from her residential care home with a young male nurse.

And Perry spent his days sitting on the daybed staring at the walls, or sitting on the floor staring at the daybed, or lying on his back staring at the ceiling, listening to the phone ring, his voice on the answering machine announcing brightly that he wasn't at home. He didn't read his mail. He didn't read the papers. He didn't even read the dozens of glossy magazines with his face beaming from the cover, which were piled up, pristine and unread, on the floor. He would look up list-lessly as his assistant appeared at irregular intervals with another strange container with another rubber body part. He would look at the accompanying photos almost indifferently, as if they were holiday snapshots an aunt was showing him. Each featured his puppet in a different location: standing on one foot beside the Eiffel Tower, waving a stump outside St. Peter's in Rome, dressed in child-sized lederhosen outside a Munich *bierkeller*, two toes stuck rakishly in its Tyrolean hat. There wasn't any ransom note. He would hand them back and go on staring at the wall.

There were rumors in the papers that due to Perry's lengthy absence his soap opera character was going to be killed off—carjacked in Florida and sent home in a box. The manager got on the phone and threatened lawsuits. A scriptwriter came up with the inspired idea of having Perry's character kidnapped by a Florida drug baron who mistook him for the son of the boss of a rival cartel. Not only would it inject some *Miami Vice* glam, but they could show his pic-ture in every episode and keep it going until Perry came back. But nothing could be done about the musical. His under-study—blond, bland and as white-bread as the music—was getting rave reviews in Perry's role, so after three months they gave him the job.

Meanwhile, several thousand miles away in Los Angeles, at five in the morning a tour bus pulls up outside Mann's Chinese Theatre. It has dark windows like cheap sunglasses and dead flies clinging to the radiator grille. In the front of the bus is a pale, English pop band; in the back, a cluster of big, black equipment flight-cases. A couple are stenciled with the name of a band: Swallow. On others the name has been spray-painted out and replaced with a new name: Femme Fatale.

Someone lifts the lid of a guitar case. Inside, wedged inside the square foam-rubber insert like an oversized turkey in a small microwave oven, its extremities either folded in or missing, is Perry's puppet. A young man—slim, good-looking, wavy-haired, pulpy-lipped—tugs out the puppet, which in its better days might well have been the Spitting Image of himself. He jumps down off the bus, two of his bandmates following. One is holding a large cardboard square with a pink star drawn on it—a homemade copy of a star on the Hollywood Walk of Fame.

He lays it out on the ground while his colleague keeps a lookout. From his pocket he takes a joke-shop dog turd, and stumbling around like a drunk with laughter, he puts it on the cardboard star, on which Perry's name is written in gold. The puppet is slumped against the wall like a beggar, gazing down at the star with its one dead eye. The bus driver jumps down, laughing, brandishing a camera. A dangerous-looking character staggering down Hollywood Boulevard, cursing at shop windows, sees them and throws them a cheery grin and waves. Back inside the bus, the bass player is sitting at a table with a penknife, prising the bottom off a domed snow globe that says "L.A. snowman"—a little top hat, cane, and carrot floating around in water. Spilling out the liquid, he plunks in the puppet's eyeball and squashes the plastic base back on.

Back in London, Perry's manager is in no mood for arguments. He's just taken on a new girl singer whose record is already tearing up the charts, whom the pop papers are calling the next big thing, and whose PMT is driving him to drink. All he needs is another moody popstar. He drives over to Perry's house, yells into the entry phone, strides in, and unrolls a chart he's made listing all the magazines and newspapers in Britain, logged with entries when anything on Perry has appeared. Blank. Nothing on the radio, nothing on the television. Perry's book is hardly selling. The soap opera contract has finally run out. Perry's last appearance was at a ratings-busting funeral, where his mates scattered his ashes at his local pub. The record company was screaming because a new album had been scheduled for the summer and Perry still hadn't written one new song. Feeling too feeble to put up a protest, Perry agreed to go into the studio and record a cover version of a maudlin hotel bar ballad. It hardly dented the charts at home but was climbing up the Top 100 in the States. MacFee had hired an L.A. publicist who had arranged a spot for Perry on the TV program *Solid Gold.* Unless Perry wanted to find a new manager, he told him—assuming he could get one—he'd better get his ass in gear.

Backstage in the green room at the Hollywood TV station, an assortment of people so disparate it's hard to believe they belong to the same species are studying a video monitor and waiting for their turn. What they are watching is a TV station floor manager with comic aspirations trying to liven up a studio audience consisting of several rows of teenagers on metal folding chairs. There are muscular women dancers in red tube tops and sequined leg warmers stretching, and an equally muscular man running through his warm-up routine with an unlit cigarette in his mouth. In one corner is an English popstar dressed in a highwayman's outfit; in another corner, a tiny American rockstar, hiding from view behind his enormous white-haired bodyguard. Perry Kaye is wandering about the room with a towel around his waist. He hasn't dressed yet. He stops and stares at himself in the mirror. The fluorescent lights are harsh. It seems to him his cheeks are beginning to sag.

Someone calls someone to call Perry in for makeup and he enters the room just as the newly oranged, pale English pop band are leaving. Their guitarist spots Perry and comes over, smiling, and slaps him on the back.

"Perry, hey, how's it going? Good to see you, man. You know, we should get together sometime, do something for old times' sake?"

As the man smiles and babbles, Perry looks at him blank-faced. Until one of his bandmates comes over, glares at Perry, puts his hand around the guitarist's shoulder, and pulls him away. It's only as Perry sits there being slapped in tan foundation that he puts a name to the face. He needs a break; he must be losing it. They'd only played in the same group together for five years. Swallow. The band he'd quit for a solo career. Perry screws up his forehead. The makeup girl complains as the foundation rises like little sandworms on his brow.

A former teen idol dressed in something uncle-y, a sweater and loose-fronted, bumpless, Ken doll pants, is standing on a stage which is dotted here and there with glittery white columns. He's reading felt-tipped clichés from cue cards that someone's holding by the camera. "You know? One of the hardest things in life is to say good-bye." Cut to Perry Kaye onstage, surrounded on all sides by columns and sequined amazons. They're playing the introduction to his mawkish remake of "Let's Just Kiss and Say Good-Bye." He glances at his feet; lifts his head, impassioned, to the ceiling; raises his arms; undulates his body slowly, first the top, then the bottom, like the two halves were on ball bearings; and fixes a seductive gaze on a young pimply girl in the studio audience who is staring at him, transfixed.

And he opens his mouth to mime to the song. And it stays open. He grinds to a halt. The producer shouts: "Cut." Perry has just seen, at the back of the studio, behind the pimply girl's head, his posterior on one of the folding chairs. Cut off clumsily at the waist and thighs, it is gyrating nonchalantly in time to the music, the left cheek pivoting coquettishly, the right executing a stately pavane.

Anyone still watching the monitor in the green room would have seen Perry collapsing into the arms of the muscular male dancer, who by now has lost the cigarette. He is led offstage, shoulders slumped, sobbing. The audience is gawking. The song goes on playing without him until someone thinks of turning the record off. And the English pop band are all falling about the room, laughing, except for the guitar player, who has a thoughtful look on his face. The drummer comes over and gives him a playful one-two punch to the chest. "Joke him," he says, "if he can't take a fuck." And the singer and the bassist strike up a singsong like drunk English football fans, the dirty version of "Amazing Grace." The guitarist laughs too now and joins in loudly. They whoop and applaud as the stagehand carries off the still-grinding rubber rump.

# TOO WEIRD FOR ZIGGY (A DREAM OF HOLES)

The party was too weird for Ziggy. "This is too weird for me, man," Ziggy said and split. It was weird, even by L.A. standards. By rock 'n' roll standards too it was weird—a party centered around a hole. Like regular parties, parties without holes, there were security men in black suits guarding the gate. Limos circled and disgorged in the driveway, valet parkers in red brocade waistcoats shunted back and forth in cars that could make you cry. Night was starting to fall, someone was lighting the outdoor heaters. Someone else was digging a hole in the sand.

At a carved wooden table on the beach sat a sharp-eyed man with wealthy skin. His shirt, despite the evening chill, was open. He was covered in chest hair; it looked like he'd walked head-on into a pube-spraying machine. "Where's Ziggy?" he said.

"He's fucked off," said an aide.

"He can fuck off then." The man frowned. "Asshole. Like he doesn't need the publicity." A sand-brown blonde stood behind him kneading his shoulders. His head was jammed back into her man-made chest like it was the headrest in his Porsche. He stared straight ahead at the man by the ocean, digging in the wet sand. The hole was now wedge-shaped, five and a half feet long, not too wide. The digger was beveling the edges, pushing the sharp edge of the shovel straight down into the sand. Nearby, a film crew erected an elaborate Meccano set of lights and microphones. If they had been any nearer they would have heard his body hair crunch under her fingers.

"Is *she* here yet?"

He couldn't see her among the party guests who were starting to spill out onto the beach. Top-of-the-range celebrities—Irving's parties were legendary—with just enough grade twos and threes to make the great feel ogled and envied and thus even greater, but not so many that they'd feel they'd been misfiled in a B-list event. Young women in tiny dresses with spaghetti straps buzzed like mosquitoes around the biggest stars.

The young man he was addressing wore petrified hair and a face frozen into a permanent state of anxiety. "Don't believe so, Irv, but I'll check." He muttered into his headset. "No she's not, but wife, excuse me widow, number one is. Just this minute arrived. Apparently she's got a camera crew with her, from CPB. They're doing a story on her life with the great man."

"Not here they're not. Tell them to get the fuck out, MTV has the exclusive." The aide spoke again into the headset, more forcefully this time. Irving watched her glide through the French doors onto the terrace, closely followed by a girl with a furry microphone on a long boom and two men with camcorders, visibily remonstrating with his staff. The Baroness's ex-wife wore an orange dress, tight as a condom. She looked magnificent. The Baroness sure could pick them, bastard, Irving thought.

"Irv, Mr. Narcisse is here," the aide announced.

"Good. Tell Kelly to bring him straight down." A sharp breeze whipped in off the water; Irving buttoned his shirt. Moments later a slim young woman with big hair appeared, leading a large black man in a verdigris cape that appeared to be made out of something lumpy and still alive, like vulture's legs. He was carrying a case. Irving got up, shook his hard brown hand, and gestured him to sit down.

"Mr. Narcisse, what can I get you?" He signaled to a drinks waiter.

"My payment. Cash. In advance."

This amused Irving. "You and Chuck Berry," he laughed, and extracted a billfold, peeled off a wodge of notes. Narcisse flicked the edges expertly before stashing them away about his person. He sat down and put his case on the table.

"Kelly, get Mr. Narcisse whatever he needs," said Irving. "Time to go meet and greet." On a stage erected on the beach a five-piece covers band, each of them dressed to reflect one of the Baroness's many stage incarnations—space alien, hermaphrodite, cowboy, gigolo, vampire—struck up one of his classic songs.

Celebrities clutching cocktail glasses milled around. Some made small talk, most just checked one another out. There were stars from the film, art, and theater world, but mostly there were musicians—fifty-something rockstars, the Baroness's contemporaries if he'd still been alive. All of them had tight pants and tighter teenage wives. Their hair tumbled to their shoulders like it was running away from the balding bit on top. There were musicians too from a younger generation whose goatees and hairdos the Baroness had happily filched. And, honoring his final incarnation as a dissipated rock 'n' roll Dracula, there was a flock of neo-goths: girls in webby black dresses and pale men thin as skewers, picking at the hollows of their cheeks with long pointy fingers and gazing like jilted heroines out to sea. Those, that is, who weren't gazing at the hole.

The TV camera sucked them all in, then swung round to close up on Churchill: MTV's current star presenter. A designer boy-poet with Byron's curls and Johnny Depp's eyes.

"Rock 'n' roll, to quote the great god Neil Young, will never die," Churchill testified. "But rock 'n' rollers?" A pause while he pulled his perfect face into a mask of tragedy. "Ah that, my friends, is a whole different story. They just keep on dying. John Lennon, Jimi Hendrix, Kurt Cobain—God sure knows how to pick a band." The upper right-hand corner of Churchill's lip started to twitch. This, the cognoscenti knew, signaled possession not by Elvis but the Spirit of Poetry. Verse was coming through.

"Mangled on the highway, disemboweled by stalkers
Fried by faulty wires, tumbling out of planes
Pierced like San Sebastian by a million hypodermics
Stardust to dust, the end of the game—or is it?

"Tonight, exclusively on MTV, you and I and a galaxy of stars will witness the making—or I should say *re*-making—of rock 'n' roll history. The ultimate comeback. Here, live on this beach in Malibu, California, at the multi-million-dollar home of legendary rock 'n' roll manager Irving Roth, one of the most influential figures the world of rock has ever known, so cruelly taken away from us last December, will stand and walk among us again. The venerable; the mythical; the forever cool, forever young, *The Baroness*. So"—

he flips a casual hand at the lens—"you say you wanna resurrection? Stick around."

Cut to the commercials: Linkin Park's retrospective ten-album box set, the latest Nike trainers, cherry-scented tampons, strawberry shampoo, 'Scream 7' and 'Aliens 8,' two for Pepsi and a plug for the upcoming MTV special, an exclusive interview with Rex on why he broke up Shoot 2 Kill.

Meanwhile Churchill pointed out the stars he wanted for sound bites. His producer noted them down meticulously on her clipboard. He looked around. "Where's Ziggy?" he asked.

"Gone," she said. "Came and went. Said it was *too weird,*" and laughed like it was the craziest thing she'd heard.

"Too weird?" he grunted. "For Ziggy? Like he just sits around in Miami reading fucking books all day? Note it down: I am *officially* pissed off."

"Okay. Pussy's just arrived though."

He looked up.

"Do you want her on the list? She's on. And don't forget the lucky winner." The producer nodded over to where an assistant was babysitting the whey-faced winner of a competititon to present the reanimated Baroness with a platinum album for one million posthumous U.S. sales of his CD *Unplugged*. Wide-eyed and trembling, the girl stared at the poet with barely disguised adoration. He flashed her his sweetest smile. "Fat slut," he muttered. "Can't they make them send in photos with their entries?" Unconsciously the girl snapped off the head of the single white lily she clutched in her hand.

The covers band had left the seventies and moved on to the Baroness's biggest hits from the eighties. A few of the celebrities had climbed onstage to jam. Their women offered up exaggerated support down below, dancing, clapping, whooping. The TV camera watched them for a while and then left them to it, heading off with Churchill for his round of interviews.

Resurrecting the Baroness, the first star told him, was a blessing. The next one said it was a curse. One called it a brilliant back-catalogue-shifting publicity stunt, another said it was a sick joke. His ex-wife wept all down her orange dress and said how much she'd loved him. The young singer with an L.A. nu-metal band put his arm across her shoulder and whispered, "You're only as dead as your last album. The Baroness *lives*."

"The Baroness," one of his many former bandmates said soberly, "was always dying and being reborn. He never lost the capacity to change and to surprise. He was a calculating man but I would say—and I don't use the term lightly—a fucking genius. The Baroness knew instinctively how to go for effect."

"The Baroness," slurred a drunker friend, "was an artist—a glorious fucking rip-off artist. He'd mug you for your ideas as soon as look at you, then squirrel them off to his bank account. A huge great stockpile of his friends' and enemies' bright, shiny ideas. But what that fucker made with them was beautiful. Beautiful." He held his hand up to the camera lens. "Turn that off, I don't want you to see me fucking cry. He was a brilliant man, the Baroness, with a wicked sense of humor. Yeah go on, dig him up. He would've appreciated it. Ziggy'll tell you—Ziggy was his best friend. Ziggy!" he shouted.

"Ziggy's fucked off," said his male companion, dragging him away. "Didn't want anything to do with it."

"I don't fucking believe you. Ziggy!"

Irving was speaking on camera. "The Baroness," he told Churchill, "was an artist in the true sense of the word. A Renaissance man in an era that rewards mediocrity. Have you ever seen his paintings? He gave me one once. He painted it in the French château where he made *Madonna of the Lipgloss*. A masterpiece. Greatest album of love songs ever made and I'll stand on John Lennon's white grand piano and say that. Legend had it that the château was haunted by the ghost of Chopin, the classical composer. The Baroness told me how he and Chopin would sit up all night playing duets and drinking the finest Bordeaux wine. So to answer your question, no, he wouldn't find this at all weird. The Baroness was no stranger to elegance and death. Now if you'll excuse me, I've got a resurrection to get on the road."

He slipped out of the lights and walked toward the house. *Madonna of the Lipgloss*, where the fuck was she? He was starting to feel anxious, and anxious was something that Irving didn't do.

The aide was on the terrace, still speaking into his headset. "We can't reach her," he said, anticipating the question. "Her cell phone's off. But Kelly managed to get hold of her housekeeper and she said she was definitely dressed for a party when she left."

Kelly anticipated the next question. "Almost two hours ago. Limo. The housekeeper didn't know which company—

the guys have been on the past half hour trying to trace it. We'll buzz you the second we know anything. I reckon we've got, uh," she looked at her watch, "fifteen minutes, twenty tops. You're on after Churchill. Mr. Narcisse is ready whenever you are."

The music had stopped playing, the band had left the stage, and Churchill had taken their place. He was reading an epic poem he had written for the occasion titled "On the Third Day.' Afterward one of the goths came up and put a skeletal arm around him. "Hey man, I always thought you were a phoney, but that was great, dude, really great." His girlfriend lifted her voluminous black skirt to reveal her mound of Venus, draped in black crepe since the Baroness's death as a mark of respect.

Then it was Irving's turn. He clicked off the cell phone in his pocket, climbed the wooden steps, and stood at the microphone in the middle of the stage, directly under the spotlight. He asked for silence. He told them why they had been invited. He spoke eloquently of the Baroness and of their "long, special relationship," of the "misunderstanding" that broke it up, and of "that wonderful week" at the family house in Switzerland where they "hugged and kissed and reconciled." And then—the spotlight turned a dramatic blue—just one month later the terrible late-night phone call. The long flight, the tears, depression, comforting the widow (ah, the widow, he thought, why hasn't she come? This was all for her, the whole fucking lot of it, the Baroness could rot in Hell for all he cared, but if that's what she wanted then goddammit, he'd go find him, fetch him back, have him stuffed and mounted in a corner of the bedroom if that's what it took for them to be together. Where the fuck is she?) The world lost a genius, he said. He lost a friend. And then one day, one incredible day, he heard about a man in New Orleans. A necromancer. A reanimator. He spent weeks tracking the man down, several more checking him out, and still more in negotiation. "And if you know me," he smiled, "and you know how I do business, then you know (the Madonna of the Lipgloss knew) that I don't take no for an answer.

"And so, ladies, gentleman, *friends*—I give you: The Return of the Baroness."

The spotlight slid away from Irving and across the beach to Narcisse, who was arranging the contents of his case on the table by the hole. One corner of the table had sagged into the sand. There was a box of matches on it, a ball of fuse wire, gaffer tape, a candle, a jar, a sponge—like one of those PBS children's TV shows where you get to make a windmill out of familiar household objects. The celebrities, who had been drifting over, now arrived en masse. The only straggler was Pussy. She was drunk and her stiletto heels had sunk into the sand. She leaned back, like a road sign warning of an upcoming hill, staring down at her glass, which sat wonkily, upturned, on the beach.

Off in the distance, a mournful New Orleans brass band was playing the Baroness's most poignant ballad as a procession made its way slowly toward the sea. An androgynous young male majorette led the parade, slowly twirling a neon tube. Close behind were four young men, slim as dancers, dressed in top hats and leotards. They shouldered a coffin covered in tiny mirror tiles that twinkled here and there like a defective mirror ball. Behind the coffin, walking gingerly on high heels and carrying a silver tray, was an enormous but graceful black drag queen. The tray held a silver mirror, champagne, and cigarettes.

The procession halted beside the hole. The coffin was gently lowered into it. The drag queen put down her tray beside the hole and dabbed her eyes dramatically with a large black lace handkerchief. The prizewinner, now nervously clutching the platinum disc, darted prematurely forward, realized her error, and froze under the spotlight. A production assistant abruptly pulled her back. The music crescendoed, then stopped.

Deathly silence. All eyes, black and widened, were on Narcisse. He was squatting by the hole. From out of his cape he took the ball of wire. He leaned down and attached one end to the coffin handle. Slowly he stood up and walked back to the table, unraveling as he went. He coiled the other end of the fuse around the candle. He gaffer-taped the candle to the tabletop. He unscrewed the jar and dipped the sponge into it. He carried the sponge carefully back to the hole. He held it high over the coffin, squeezed it six times, then stopped. Six more, a pause, then another six.

He shot around suddenly as a woman rushed into the camera lights. She was statuesque, sad-eyed, with oversized, slick, incandescent lips. Visibly distressed, she thrust a fur coat into Narcisse's hand. "He'll be cold," she told him, "he'll want this," then she turned and hurried off.

Irving spotted her from the stage. He cried out her name but she didn't hear him; the microphone had been turned off. He tried to keep sight of her as she moved further from the camera lights and into the darkness. He ran down the steps and dashed toward the spot where he last saw her go. Narcisse lay the expensive coat down by the water. The sea sucked greedily at one arm. He stared briefly into the hole, muttered something that wasn't English, and walked back to the table.

Narcisse struck a match and lit the candle. The flame leaned sideways in the breeze, pulled itself back upright, then went out. The crowd exhaled. One of Irving's aides ran over and wedged some big stones around the sinking table leg—awkwardly, since everyone was watching. Everyone except Irving, who was now some distance down the beach. He was on his knees in the cold sand, his feet in the lapping water, shoulders stooped, face buried in the stomach of the tall, thin woman with the shiny mouth. She stood there, motionless. At a distance their conjoined silhouettes looked like the buttress and wall of a church.

Narcisse looked over at them briefly, his face impassive. Then he turned back to the table. Casually he struck another match. The flame hovered for a moment, flared, then bit into the top of the fuse. It snaked swiftly down and around the candle. Spitting and sparking, it hissed along the wire toward the wet, black hole.

# JEREMIAH 18:1-10

We were in the hotel bar after the show, it was just gone two, you could see that the bartender was impatient to go home but, hey, only four more hours till our flight so no point going to bed. There were six of us—me and my photographer, Eric; Jerry and Ted from *XO* magazine; Paul from *Hundred% Heavy*; and Rollo, the publicist, the man who'd brought us all over to the States and was right now buying drinks at the bar. All of a sudden this girl comes up on my blind side and taps me on the shoulder and says in a soft Southern accent, "Pardon me, are you with the band?"

"Certainly is," Eric shot back. "Shoot 2 Kill's chief knob-sucker. Four foot tall, no teeth—made for the job." "Fuck you," I said with no particular malice. Photographers are all sociopaths—something to do with always looking at the world through a lump of glass—plus it was as good an answer as any to the "Are you with the band?" question that rock journalists are always asked.

"Only," she continued, undaunted for someone who looked so small and meek, "I saw you backstage earlier talking to Rex."

"She's doing a story for *Pulp*," said Rollo, "June issue, cover, double spread." Like all publicists, he couldn't go long without telling everyone what a good job he was doing. The girl ignored him. "Do you know Duggsy?" she asked. She meant John Dugsdale, Shoot 2 Kill's drummer.

"Everyone knows Duggsy," Jerry said, chuckling. "Genius! The star of the show!"

"You know, God's a good bloke," Eric joined in, "only he does keep thinking he's Duggsy." The girl just looked perplexed.

"Modesty," Eric explained, "is not Duggsy's strongest suit."

"Neither's drumming," I said, and we all fell about in exaggerated drunken laughter. Except the girl. She just stood there with her thin hair and long, baggy sweater and pale, waxy face and said in a pained voice, "Do you know where I can find him?"

Just then two of the band's roadies walked into the bar. "Hey!" shouted the fat one in the faded black Aerosmith T-shirt. "It's the snorkeling Southerner. Back for another mouthful, darling?"

"Our cocks," said the other in a bad fake-posh English accent, "are quite frankly irresistible." He had scrawny gray hair that stuck out from his bald patch and disgusting trousers whose crotch dangled close to his knees.

"She wants to know where the drummer is," said Eric. "Last time I looked," said Disgusting Trousers, "he was backstage in a room with a camcorder and two naked birds on the concrete floor, stoned as fuck, eating each other out." I don't know what she wanted to hear but it wasn't this. The girl visibly crumpled. She ran out of the bar. I felt bad. I almost went after her—she had that innocence about her that the Japanese girl fans have; it makes you want to protect them. But there are certain rules of rock journalism that are inviolable, chief among them abandoning the bar when someone's getting in the drinks, and anyhow I didn't want to give the boys any excuse to go thinking I was soft.

"Mad cunt," said Aerosmith. He told us they'd found her hovering by the pit when the show was over while they were doing the rounds with backstage passes, trawling for blondes who wanted to meet the band. "She comes up to me and says she has to see the *drummer*. So I say"—he knocks back a beer, a good third of it spilling onto his T-shirt and softening up a blob of what I hoped was mashed potato on his chest—"you know the routine. Only apparently she doesn't. Though her being blonde and female and breathing, naturally, we figure that she does."

As a point of information for females, this is the basics of the Backstage Pass Transaction. A sordid business. In a nutshell: They've got something you want (band access), you've got something they want (XX chromosomes), and so a deal is struck. To get to the vocalist you fuck the tour manager; for the guitarist you blow two roadies; for the bass player you blow one; and if it's the drummer you're after they'll send you off for a brain scan, bum a cigarette, and give you an Access All Areas. Drummers, you might have gathered, do not rate high in the rock pecking order. Neither, for that matter, do girls.

"So, when the dirty deed is done I ask her what the fuck she wants with the *drummer*. I tell her that there was this drummer one time who was touring with Alice Cooper and Alice's rattlesnake gets out of its snake box backstage and bites him on the dick. And there's this rancid old groupie wandering around the corridors looking for famous knobs to suck and the drummer yells for her to go and get the doctor. So she goes to the doctor's and tells him the drummer's been bitten on his dick by a snake. There's just one cure, the doctor tells her: Suck out the venom or he'll die. So she goes back." He fell about laughing. "And the drummer says, well what did the doctor say? And she says—"

Paul interrupted: "'The doctor says you're going to die!' Come on, that's an antique." Aerosmith was choking with laughter, tears rolling down his cheeks. If you didn't know better you might have thought he was crying.

"And," he managed to get out between gasps, "the girl doesn't even *smile*. She says, she's going to *marry* him. That she's had a message from *God*. I say, 'Why the hell would God want you to marry Duggs? Fucking Jesus, he must have it in for you.'" Duggsy already has three ex-wives—and three jail terms for assault and battery. Plus an ongoing lawsuit from an ex-girlfriend, the mother of his child, who says he abused their little girl. Duggsy hits things. He's a drummer.

"And *she* says"—he rolled his eyes to heaven—"'It is not for me to question God.'"

"Wicked!" Rollo grinned.

"Top five lies told by drummers!" announced Paul. Uh-oh, circle joke. "Number five: I taught John Bonham everything he knew. "Four," the guy from *XO* joined in, "I practice eight hours a day." "Three," yelled Eric—why do men get so excited over lists?—"I'm on the cover of *Modern Drummer* any day now." "Two," guffawed Paul, "they'd never fire me. I hold the band together." Aerosmith nodded, and said, "Good one." "Number one," said Rollo, "my girlfriend's a supermodel." "Nah," screamed Disgusting

Trousers, "she's a fucking great singer and the record label has asked me to produce her album!"

Whoever Duggsy's girlfriend might be, one thing was for sure: She was not going to be a timid girl with a flat chest on a mission from God.

Up all night and still we managed to get to the airport late, so I found myself stuck in a middle seat on the plane next to a stranger. Turned out he had been staying in our hotel. Somewhere over the Atlantic he told me about this strange thing that happened to him the previous night. There was a knock on his door. He was fast asleep, disoriented, and got up and opened it without thinking and the girl from the bar walked straight in. It was two-thirty in the morning, she was dressed, he wasn't, apart from his underpants, and the etiquette of the situation left him at a disadvantage. And he could see she was upset. Plus I guess he saw something in her face, just like I did. She sat on the edge of his bed, back straight, hands in her lap, rubbing one thumb slowly around the other, while he went and grabbed the toweling robe from the edge of the tub. She told him she'd had a bad experience but she was all right now. She said her name was Jeanie and she that she taught English as a foreign language. She asked to use the bathroom and he couldn't see how he could say no.

She was in there almost an hour. Finally he rapped on the door and asked if she was okay, scared to death at what he would find. Only she came out and with a little smile said, "I'm fine. Thank you, you've been very kind." And then she left. He went back to bed but of course he couldn't sleep, all he could do was lie there. It was only when he used the bathroom once he got up that he saw what she'd been doing.

It was the toilet roll. It was covered from beginning to end with neat handwriting. The whole thing, written on and wound up again. He'd flushed the first few sheets down the pan before he'd noticed it but he could just make out the heading on the mangled top-sheet: "Message From God." He sat back down and tugged on the rest of the roll. There was a detailed account of when and where she got her epiphany, a long and intricate treatise on why she was chosen, some verses from the Bible—Jeremiah 18, he remembered it said, verses 1 to 10—and what appeared to him to be an original love sonnet in the Elizabethan tradition. On the last sheet was the message: "To the Maid, Rm 2021 Lexus Inn, from Miss Jeanie Jackson. Please deliver this to hotel guest Mr. J. Dugsdale (registered under the name Mr. Hugh G. Reckshun)."

"What did you do with it?"

"I left it," he said. "I don't suppose you have any idea who this Dugsdale character is?"

Back in London, eight weeks later Shoot 2 Kill were over on the U.K. leg of their tour. It was then that I saw her again, Wembley Arena, second row, eyes fixed on Duggsy like a zoom lens with a mouth on the end sucking him in. When I went backstage afterward to say hi to the band, she wasn't there. Disgusting Trousers was, though, one hand clamped around a can of beer, the other patting a blonde girl's arse. The blonde didn't seem to notice. She had her sights on Rex, who'd just stepped out of his dressing room, and without a word to the roadie she charged in his direction.

"How do you do, my little friend from the fourth estate," the roadie greeted me in that dreadful Monty Python upper-class accent. "You'll simply never guess who was here. Remember that unfortunate young lady from the Long Beach show, the one so enamored of Mr. Dugsdale?"

"You mean Saint Duggsy of the Sacred Drumstick?"

"Indeed."

"I saw her in the crowd," I said. "Is she still on her mission from God?"

"She is."

"And how is it progressing?"

"Well, Sir Duggs unfortunately was unable to talk to her. He's got his mouth full"—he gestured toward a dressing room. "He's back there with his wife du jour, Amber Lee." Registering my blank look, he made the internationally recognized gesture of extremely large breasts and licked his lips. "Stripper. Sadly, Amber found her own way backstage so I was unable to grease her for him first. Well, must run, toodle pip," he said, and sauntered off.

And that's when I spotted her. She was sitting on a flight-case, talking to the wardrobe girl. They were laughing like old friends. "Look," I said to Eric when he came out of the guitarist's dressing room, three big cameras draped around his neck. She hadn't noticed me. She was concentrating on helping fold away the sweaty stage clothes into their respective boxes. "Ah, the future Mrs. Dugsdale," Eric beamed and began snapping at her with his long lens.

You come across a lot of nuts in this line of work—"superfans," I believe is the polite term. More men than girls, it might surprise you to know, and normally it's the singer who gets them, though I met a guy once who claimed that every time the bass player of Earthkwake had an orgasm no matter where he was he came too. But you can usually spot them a mile off, and little Jeanie Jackson just didn't look like one. Too sensible. Though her blowing two roadies to meet a borderline psycho drummer under divine injunction doesn't help my argument. Still, she seemed to have got in with the band's wardrobe girl, which is a pretty smart move if you want to meet a band. And, I don't know, she just intrigued me.

Then, a few days later, Eric showed me the contact sheet. The series of tiny black-and-whites clearly showed her reaching into the flight-case marked in big white letters "DUGGSY" when the wardrobe girl wasn't looking and taking something out. A black book—a Filofax maybe. Next picture it's vanished and she's back folding things again.

There hadn't been any good stalker stories in the Sundays for an age and I figured that Jeanie might make a good one: Suburban teacher falls for big-time star, ditches her fiancé, abandons her students—leaving them wandering the town like zombies babbling in bad pidgin English with nowhere to turn for help—takes all her savings out of the bank, and follows Duggsy around the world from show to show, sleeping on the floor outside his hotel room. You could write it without having to interview her. But just for the hell of it I had a go at tracking her down. I e-mailed the tour manager—the tour by now had moved on to Europe— but he said there had been no sign of her at any of the shows. She'd probably given up and gone home, he said, which is exactly what the band was going to do after its German dates.

I checked out the Shoot 2 Kill sites on the Net—plenty of crackpot fans, but no Jeanie Jackson. Then, like any self-respecting rock journalist, I gave up, had a drink, and moved on to another story.

In the end *she* found *me*. Around nine months later—the same day the newspapers announced that Duggsy and his "dancer girlfriend Amber" planned to tie the knot in Hawaii—I got home to find a message from her on my answering machine. A chiming Southern voice I recognized at once as Jeanie's said, "Hi, my name is Angie Carson. You don't know me but John Dugsdale of Shoot 2 Kill gave me your number. There is something important I would like to speak with you about. I'll try calling again later." And she did—a short conversation in which "Angie" arranged to meet me the following afternoon at a coffee bar in Soho.

The place was one of those old Italian jobs that the Starbucks and Coffee Republics hadn't quite managed to elbow out. Formica tables, thick white cups with coffee stains etched into the cracks in the china, and a clientele roughly divided between media types in black and Italian blokes who looked like they were on their tea break from a low-budget Mafia film. I was impressed that Jeanie knew the place; she must have been in town for a while. She was already there when I arrived, sitting in the corner clutching a coffee.

She looked different—her hair was blonder, or worn differently maybe, so that it accentuated her eyes. Though she still wore leggings and a big, loose, pastel sweater, on a gray day in a London café they looked less pathetic, less out of place than among the tight bright spandex and fake glamour of backstage. Anyhow, her air of vulnerability had gone—though she still looked very young, twenty-five tops, an American twenty-five the rough equivalent of a sixteen-year-old Londoner. When she saw me come through the door, she looked shocked. I guess when she'd called she'd had no idea that the person on the other end of the phone was the journalist she'd met in Long Beach; she evidently thought I was just another of the long list of girls in Duggsy's life. I ordered a coffee at the counter and sat down opposite her.

"Thank you for coming" was all she said. She would not look me in the eye, just stared at her cup. I didn't say anything—old journalist trick: I wanted her to be the one to break the silence—but she looked like she'd be content just sitting there forever swirling the coffee around and around. So I asked her why she called me. After quite a long while she answered, "It's complicated." I said Duggsy didn't give her my number, she hadn't even met Duggsy, had she, and she went pale. I'd figured out that the book she'd lifted from Duggsy's case must have been his address book, and I confronted her with it. She confessed at once, almost gratefully, telling me how bad she felt about committing a sin. She launched into a long, convoluted explanation—like she was explaining one of the more complicated forms of English grammar to her students—which boiled down to the fact that they're God's commandments and if He wanted them broken, then what was she to do? I asked her if she'd been ordered to break any others and she smiled sadly and shook her head.

She took the book out of her bag and put it on the table between us, looking at it as if it would walk away from her and sort everything out by itself. I asked her again why she'd phoned me and she said she had been trying to get in touch with everyone in the book. She'd already managed to talk to a good three-quarters of the names—on the phone mostly; she only had so much money for airfares and very few of them wanted to meet up. What did she want from them? I asked, and she said she wanted to know what their relationship with Duggsy was like—no, really she wanted to know all about *him:* what he did, what he said to them, how he felt about things, what his life was like. Everything.

Most of them, as you'd have guessed, were girlfriends of the extremely part-time variety. Several had geographical locations and days of the week scribbled by their names, or what might have been codes for their sexual specialties. She phoned the numbers and told them she was the band's personal assistant and that they were arranging a surprise party for Duggsy, to which of course the girl in question would be invited. They had given her the job of secretly finding out what Duggsy was into, his likes and dislikes, so they could buy him something a bit more personal than a cymbal and some gold-plated drumsticks. Occasionally she changed the story: She'd been hired to write Shoot 2 Kill's official biography and Duggsy had specifically requested that she interview the girl in question about the details of their relationship.

She called Duggsy's parents and told them her name was Amber—they'd seen pictures of their son's fiancée in the papers but had never actually met her—and she charmed them into talking to her about him at length. They told her what he was like as a child, even told her his health problems.

They sent her photos of themselves with Duggsy as a little boy. Armed with these, she was able to pass herself off to other people as his sister. And they believed her. Hell, I almost believed her too. And she even managed to persuade Duggsy's ex-girlfriend Stephanie—the one who had taken out the child abuse suit—to invite her into the house. Jeanie had hidden a miniature Dictaphone in her pocket and planned to trick Stephanie into admitting on tape that Duggsy was innocent, then take the tape to the cops. But Stephanie kept on saying such dreadful things about him that she slapped her. Stephanie screamed. Neighbors called the police. Jeanie was thrown in a cell.

"The worst thing was they wouldn't let me keep his picture with me," she said. She took it out of her handbag. It reminded me of the pictures of rockstars that I'd had as a teenager, carefully cut from a magazine but creased and thin from frequent fingering and kissing. Duggsy looked like a tattooed broom in a baseball cap, a thin wet black ponytail flopping through the gap at the back. In the end Stephanie didn't press charges—I guess she felt sorry for Jeanie too—and Jeanie was out the next day. She went back to the house that night and spray-painted the words "God alone judges" on Stephanie's garage door.

But what I still couldn't figure out was, Why *Duggsy?* After grilling her for the best part of an hour I was still none the wiser. No, she didn't want to save him, she said; God alone could save. It wasn't sex—she had a perfectly nice boyfriend, thank you—and it wasn't looks; apparently the perfectly nice boyfriend beat him there hands down too. It certainly wasn't the music—she said she loathed heavy metal. That first time we met in Long Beach was the very first rock concert she'd been to. At first she couldn't bear it, but, baptized in the sweat that flew off Duggsy's tattooed arms as he thrashed away at the drum kit, she knew—not that she had ever doubted Him—that God had been right. Her eyes, shiny with joy, gazed past me to some distant place where she and Duggsy would sit side by side on the Eternal Drum platform at the feet of the Almighty.

Poor delusional cow, I thought. I said my good-byes and good lucks and got the hell out, planning to e-mail Shoot 2 Kill's management as soon as I got home to warn the band to be on nut alert. But I'm ashamed to say I didn't get around to it. I only remembered a couple of months later, after Duggsy was all over the tabloids in a wedding suit and baseball cap. A baffled look on his face, he stood brideless under a flowered canopy next to a Hawaiian priest. The headline read: "Rock Bad Boy's No Show Blow." But it was the story on the front page of the next day's papers that made me go cold.

They found Amber's body in a cheap apartment hotel in Honolulu. A friend of hers had come by the office, the manager said, and paid for two weeks up front, cash—guy, girl, he didn't remember, but his wife did and it was definitely a woman. His wife hadn't seen her but they'd spoken on the telephone—she told her that they didn't want maid service and that they needed to be alone because her friend had some big problems to sort out. She figured they were lesbians, not that it was any of her business. Then maybe that she *did* have problems and it was suicide. Though the fact that Amber was slit head to foot and skinned didn't particularly point to that conclusion. I couldn't stop thinking of Jeanie slipping into Amber's flesh and turning up at the wedding, popping out at kiss-the-bride time like a little Russian doll.

I scrambled around on my desk and on the floor to see if I could find the piece of paper I'd written her phone number on. Finally I did, and I dialed. I was surprised that my hand was shaking. I had no idea what I would say. "We're sorry," said an android voice, "your call cannot be completed as dialed." I called international directory; there was no listing for a Jeanie Jackson or Angie Carson in Long Beach or Los Angeles or the dozen other U.S. cities I persuaded them to try. Nothing. I called Eric and got his answering machine. Then I called my editor. He asked me if I'd heard the news: Duggsy had been taken in for questioning; with his history of violence against women, it was no great shock.

A couple of years later, I was back in Long Beach, this time to do a story on Wet Dream. Same old arena; different roadies handing out passes after the show to girls. Backstage was smokier than Keith Richards's lungs and Wet Dream was busy doing the old grip-and-grin, obligingly wrapping tattooed arms around men in designer jeans and logoed jackets who worked for the record company, radio, and TV. A balding promo guy who'd found just enough hair to drag back into a ponytail was hurling superlatives at the band. "That was the greatest, man. You were kill. Fucking brilliant. You guys kicked serious ass." They'd have kicked him off of *Spinal Tap* for overdoing it. Backstage really is the most boring place in the world. I looked around for the iced-beer bin and grabbed myself a bottle, then slipped out past the impenetrable crowd of freeloaders protesting that their name most definitely was on the VIP list and roadies running about with equipment. I sat with my beer on a box by the truck-loading bay, welcoming the cold rush of air through the open door, until a crew member came over and ushered me off.

"Wardrobe!" he yelled. "How're we doing there? Any cases ready to go? What *is* the new girl's name?" He was asking me the question, as if by mere intuitive femaleness I should know the answer. "I can't keep up with them. Just got used to the last one and she gets pregnant and fucks off."

"Hey there." The tour manager came striding over to me, waving a sheet of fax paper at me and smiling. We've bumped into each other backstage off and on for years. "Don't say I don't give you anything." He handed me the fax, and under the management's letterhead I read: "Dear Harry, Effective next Tuesday, 25th, Aaron Pike in the dumper, Duggs Dugsdale in. Official press release out Friday. Don't let it drive you to drink. Mitch."

"Duggsy of Shoot 2 Kill is joining Wet Dream?" I gasped. "Is he out then?" Last I heard he was still in pokey—got six months in Stephanie's domestic abuse case. He'd never been charged with Amber's murder, though. No one had.

The tour manager nodded. "Certainly is. A new man, I believe," he said, rolling his eyes as he took back the fax. "Oh well, I'd better get busy ordering up the video booth equipment." When I looked askance he added, "Duggsy's new hobby. You don't want to know. But just in case, as I can see from your eyes, you do, it encompasses the Dugsdale holy trinity of girls, cameras, and onanism. Right, back to work. Stay out of trouble." As he turned to go he shouted over to the roadie, "The new girl's name, as I've told you a dozen times already, is Jeanie."

"Wardrobe, ready to go!" a sweet, bright Southern accent called.

# THE AUDIENCE ISN'T LISTENING

"You're not listening."

She was. She just didn't give a fuck; she had things of her own to worry about. She lay on her back on the super-king-size bed like an effigy, eyes closed, hands across her chest. Adam sat on the edge of the bed, smoking a cigarette. A tear in the corner of the blackout blind let in a clot of smoggy afternoon sun that spotlit the guitar propped in the corner. There was something childish about his self-absorption; there was nothing maternal about her. Her big fake breasts were as hard as her heart. She knew what he was going to say anyway. Ants.

"Something's gonna have to be done about those fucking ants!"

She opened her eyes slowly. Adam wasn't there. There was a cone of cigarette smoke pointing at the hole in the blind. She stared at it for a few moments blankly and then he reappeared, like a conjuring trick, leaning over the bed. He looked smaller than he did onstage—looked actually like he had been bigger once but had been reduced in size for convenience. "They're all over the fucking snakes! Thousands of them. On their heads, in their mouths, all over their fucking eyes. I don't believe it! I told you to call pest control."

"I did. You also told me, 'Tell them not to spray anywhere near the snakes.' So I did. And they didn't." Matter-of-fact, bored even. He couldn't engage her. The audience wasn't listening. He stormed into the wings.

The phone rang. She rolled over onto her stomach and picked it up, tugged up the antenna, speaking in the same flat voice. "Yeah? No, he's busy. Squashing ants. That's what I said. In the serpentarium. With his fingers, one by one. How the hell do I know? Hours I suppose—there's thousands of them. Adam!" she yelled over the sound of running water. "Coz. Telephone." Coz was Shoot 2 Kill's manager. "He's not answering," she said. "Okay, I'll tell him." She hung up and rolled on her back again, staring at the sunbeam on the guitar neck, distractedly stroking her tiny stomach.

Before she married Adam, Gerri was a model like all the other rockstars' wives, "model" being a generic Los Angeles term for any woman who got paid to take her clothes off. Adam, like all the other rockstar husbands, had upgraded her with every rise in fortune. Her long legs were lipoed, her lips collagened, her nose clipped, her hair bleached, streaked, and extended; her breasts now stood at a top-of-the-market 38 double-F, exactly like all the other rockstar wives. They all saw the same cosmetic surgeon, worked out at the same gym. If you stacked them in a row they'd all match exactly, like paper dolls, or reflections of reflections in a mirror that went on forever.

The phone rang again. "Just thought you should know," said Coz, "I'm wise to you. Keep the fuck away from Rex. You hear me?" She went cold, sat bolt upright, staring at the bedroom door as if Adam was standing there and could hear everything. "I don't know what the hell you are talking about," she said. She wanted to hang up, but the phone stayed glued to her ear. "Find someone else to fuck. That's all. Not that it's my business, but you might try your husband.

And don't forget to tell him to call me. Urgent." He hung up. She lay there shaking, still holding the telephone, listening to silence and to the blood shrieking in her ears.

"I don't fucking believe it!" said Adam, walking into the bedroom, wearing a pair of wet black boxer shorts and clutching his cell phone. "Howie's not there." Howie was the snake man, an English expat with a long list of rockstar clients who came by once a week to clean and feed the snakes in an old pickup truck packed with live rabbits and mice. He called it Squeals On Wheels. "He'll call back," said Gerri, guilt making her momentarily solicitous. "His machine's not on and his cell's not taking messages and his paging service says he's been cut off for nonpayment. Fuck!" As if to contradict him, his mobile rang suddenly. "Hey, man, it's Joss," she could hear from where she was lying. Bass players always had loud voices, as if they refused to be ignored offstage like they always were on. "Can I come by?" he asked. "Right now is not a good time, Joss," said Adam. "Man, it's important," she heard Joss whine. "Look, I'm just pulling into your road." And she rolled her eyes, pissed off at Adam on principle at Joss's arrival while gratified that she had an excuse to be more pissed off at Adam than he had every right to be at her. She got up, pulled on yesterday's T-shirt, and went downstairs.

She took a half-gallon carton of juice from the fridge and poured herself a glass, grabbed a blueberry muffin from the open pack on the kitchen counter, and took them to the sofa. Picking up the remote, she turned the TV on and sat back, tugging the T-shirt over her bent knees. On a screen as big as that of the average suburban multiplex cinema was a huge white woman in a cheap red satin blouse telling the talk show host that she had been in McDonald's when that guy let loose with the Uzi and redecorated the place with a dozen people's guts. The bullet hit the crucifix she wore around her neck and branded its shape right between her breasts. Gerri heard Joss's Jeep pull up in the drive, heard him knock at the door, stayed sitting. The woman on the television lifted up her shirt to show the studio audience, and they all gasped as the camera closed up on two huge white mounds, made modest for American TV with what looked like black duct tape, and the red-brown, angry-looking cross that stood between them. Joss knocked again, less patiently.

"Are you gonna get the fucking door or what?" Adam called from the upstairs bathroom. She sighed and got up and, without taking her eyes off the television or her mouth off the blueberry muffin, opened the door, left it ajar, and went back to the sofa, leaving Joss to let himself in. "Fine thanks, Gerri, and how are you?" Joss said sarcastically, to no effect. Adam ran down the stairs in cutoffs and a black unbuttoned cotton shirt.

"Joss, man." He grasped his bandmate's shoulder. Glancing over at his wife and back at Joss with one of those incomprehensible looks by which men communicate that the woman in question is probably on the rag, he said, "You could fix us some coffee—if it's not too much trouble. Come on back," he said to Joss, leading him out to his studio by the pool, stopping on the way to grab a couple of beers from the fridge.

"Look, man," said Joss when they were out of earshot, "I'm sorry to come at a bad time or whatever." "Hey, no, forget it," said Adam, perched on a stool by his computer, flicking the mouse automatically to make the winged Marshall-amp screensaver disappear from the screen. "Sorry I went off on one earlier—you know, domestic shit. Good to see you; I've been working on some songs—you can help. In fact, I was thinking only this morning how much I kinda miss when we all had no money and shared a place. Fuck, was that a great time? I think it's when the tour is over, you know, I just can't adjust to being at home again. You know, it's so *Spinal Tap*. I come home and dial 9 on my phone for a line. I wake up and roll over to see who the fuck I slept with and it's my wife." They laughed, then fell silent.

"So, man, what's up?" asked Adam. "You said it was important." Joss stared at the bottle, rubbing off the label with the hard skin on his forefinger. "Rex and Deanne are getting back together," he said finally.

"Wow," said Adam. "After what Rex did to her? He must be shitting himself, the lucky fuck. He could have been facing ten years if she'd gone through with the lawsuit. Now maybe we can get on with the album. Great fucking news, man."

"It isn't," said Joss. "She said she'll take him back on one condition. That he breaks up the band."

"No!" said Adam. "And he told her to fuck off, right?"

"No," said Joss.

The two of them sat there staring at the floor. Adam had known all day that something wasn't right, but he didn't know what it was. A sick premonition of something. Now that he knew what it was he wasn't quite sure what to make of it. It was all over. He pushed the computer's backspace button as if he could wipe out the day and start over again.

Gerri came in with the coffee. She had changed into a tight pink spandex exercise top and tracksuit bottoms, her expression as impenetrable as the snakes'. "I've called the fumigators and they can come tomorrow but they said no way will they work with the snakes here so they'll have to go to the vets for a couple of nights. I've left the numbers by the kitchen phone so you'd better call them. And call Coz back; he says it's urgent. I'm going to the gym with Cathy." Cathy was Joss's ex-girlfriend. Joss sent a silent prayer of thanks to God that he hadn't married her. Wives really fucked up a band.

Cathy was already on the StairMaster when Gerri got there—one of seven women and three men in a row, the men with dark stains on the back of their tank tops, all lined up, legs choreographically pumping, staring at the bank of television sets on a scaffold in the center of the ceiling, all of which were tuned to MTV—pointless really, when you couldn't hear a thing above the blaring workout music and the grinding of machines. Cathy waved at her, and glared at the man on the StairMaster next to her, willing him to get off. Gerri shrugged and did her stretches until the machine two away from Cathy's became free, then hopped up, soon catching up speed, shouting over the head of the guy in the middle, who steadfastly held his ground.

Then Cathy pointed at the screen. It was an old Poison video. The two women screamed—between them they'd been with most of the band. Cut to Beavis and Butt-Head sniggering on the sofa. "Are they, like, girls or guys?" "Whatever they are they suck." Cathy shouted above the gym noise, "Girls I'd say. How about you, Gerri?" Gerri squealed with laughter. "*And* they suck." The guy in the middle finally gave up and climbed down from the StairMaster, tutting dramatically as he left. Next up was a band Gerri didn't recognize, Cathy either, though she said the singer was megacute so she'd make a point of finding out. Then there were ads that went on forever before Cathy said, "Look."

It was a Shoot 2 Kill video. Rex and Adam were standing together at one microphone like Siamese twins, both bare-chested and in low-slung leather pants, but it was Rex's body Gerri stared at. She couldn't wait to smear herself all over it again. Fuck Coz. Fuck Deanne. Fuck Adam. She stepped a little harder.

"Why the fuck would he want to go solo?" Adam was whingeing. "He'll never find anyone like us to play with. I mean this fucking band, this fucking band, it's *more* than just a band, man." Joss nodded. They had drunk themselves beyond self-pity into sentimentality. They were blood brothers, one body five vital organs, all for one and one for all till death do us part. They'd called Coz but all he did was confirm that it was over. He would be managing Rex. And though of course he'd do all he could to help set them up, he felt it was in their best interests and his if they looked for new management. Joss was sober enough then to mention lawsuits. Or maybe carrying on the band with a different singer. Coz said forget it, Rex's team of lawyers had gone to court and he had 100 percent rights to the name. Rex was Shoot 2 Kill, Shoot 2 Kill was Rex, and Rex could do what the fuck he wanted so he had.

Adam put down his bottle and made a decision. "I'm going to see him. We gotta talk." "I'm coming too, man," said Joss. "Shit, I'm too wasted to drive." "Me too, man. Hey, let's call Duggs," he said, suddenly remembering they had a drummer. "Duggsy's in England," said Joss. "He's guesting on Wet Dream's record." "Oh yeah, that's right," said Adam. "I'll call Gerri. She can drive us." He dialed her cell phone and got the voice mail.

Gerri was in the changing room at the gym, talking on the phone to Rex. "I want to come over," she said. "It's not a good idea," he replied. "Why not," she sneered, "Deanne?"

"No," he said evenly, "not Deanne."

"Well, I know you're getting back with her." There was triumph in her voice.

"She is my wife," Rex said nonchalantly.

"And what am I, your fucking whore?" A couple of women changing their clothes stopped what they were doing to look at her.

"No," said Rex, still calm. "You are my current guitar player's wife and a hell of a fuck."

"Is Deanne there now?"

"No, I believe she is visiting her psychiatrist."

"Then I'm coming over. I'll be there in ten."

"Do you love me?" Gerri asked as she stripped to her underwear. "No," Rex answered, "but right now I want you." He didn't tell her why he wanted her; it wouldn't have gone down too well. He had decided that he would have her the night Shoot 2 Kill played the L.A. Forum, the night Adam took it into his head to leap into the crowd. Just unclipped his guitar, put it on the ground, and, legs together, bounded over the top of it like the stage was a diving board. The fans went crazy—they hadn't found themselves that close to a member of Shoot 2 Kill for years. They passed Adam back and forth across the arena over their heads in an orderly fashion, like ants carrying crumbs, until their manager sent security in after him and they lugged him back onstage. Adam, his shirt torn off, hair all over the place, stood there grinning and gave a deep, exaggerated bow. The place went wild. Rex was furious. Deanne had learned that he was the alpha male, and now it was Adam's turn.

Deanne had become way too independent, with her kickboxing lessons and her going back to school, telling him she was sick of doing nothing but going to the gym and the hairdresser while he was out on the road and she wanted a job of her own. He pointed out slowly and methodically, like she was mentally impaired, how much money he was making. She said it was crazy that she'd spent all this time and money looking good just so she could marry someone rich enough to give her the time and money to make herself look good and it was bullshit. But then she got pregnant, which changed everything. He told her she would have to go to Arkansas and stay with his mom until the baby was born, L.A. was not a safe place for the mother of his child, with him being on the road. As for the kickboxing, forget it; he didn't want a baby with a dent in its fucking head. But Deanne was disrespectful. He almost thrashed her until he remembered that his kid was in there and let her go. It was two days before she came home—the housekeeper called and he drove straight back from the studio. She was tossing stuff into an overflowing suitcase on their bed.

"Put it back, you're going nowhere."

"Fuck you, Neanderthal!"

He turned the suitcase upside down. Its contents spilled onto the carpet.

"I said you're going nowhere with my fucking kid."

"It's not yours," she said. He finally beat the truth out of her; it was her kickboxing teacher's. Okay, so he should have called an ambulance instead of locking her in the bathroom when she started hemorraghing, but nothing he had done to her was as bad as what she had done to him. He was out of his fucking mind with grief. He didn't imagine that she'd bothered to tell the lawyers that the whole fucking time, four days and nights, he had sat on the other side of the bathroom door, weeping his fucking heart out.

He fucked Gerri fast and hard. She didn't come. She'd left by the time the limo pulled up and Adam and Joss staggered out.

Early the following morning Adam woke up with a screaming headache. He could barely walk; either his feet or the ground seemed to have disappeared. Gerri was sleeping deeply. She smelt of sex, though he was so out of it when he got home he couldn't recall doing it, though he remembered wanting to fuck her violently, take control of something in his life. But all he could think of was ants scurrying out of her pubic hair and marching in neat columns down her thighs. Shaking with nausea, he made his tentative way downstairs and took a beer from the fridge. The cold liquid made him feel a little steadier. He saw the note on the counter with the fumigator's number written on it. Shit, he thought.

He hadn't called. Clutching his bottle, he went back upstairs to the serpentarium. The snakes were lying coiled and still. There were ants everywhere.

One by one he gently lifted the snakes up and carried them into the shower. Downstairs in the kitchen he put on a kettle. He took a bag of sugar from the cupboard and brought it upstairs, pouring a long white line on the serpentarium floor. "Come on, you fuckers," he whispered, and closed the door. Back in the kitchen, waiting for the kettle to boil, he searched for saucepans to boil more water, but there weren't any. Why the hell weren't there any fucking saucepans in the kitchen! Then he thought about it: Gerri didn't cook, they hadn't eaten at home since he'd bought the place, and he guessed she hadn't either when he was away on tour. He put water in the coffee-maker and in the cappuccino machine and switched them on.

He carried the kettle of boiling water carefully up the stairs. His head pounded. The sugar he'd put down was black with ants, clambering all over each other, those at the top tumbling to the bottom of the pile and starting the climb again.

"Gotcha!" Adam said, and poured on the boiling water. Scrunched-up ant bodies floated down to the moat in great puddles of steam. Wonderful; such a feeling of release. He had to pull himself away to go fetch the rest of the water that was boiling downstairs. When he came back up with more, everything was still, like a stadium after the crowds had gone home. He was struck with a nagging feeling that there was something he hadn't done. He didn't know what it was; there was someone on the payroll to do everything. *Was.* What the fuck was he going to do now?

Gerri was still asleep. He opened the blind so that the light would wake her. Then he lay down naked on the bed next to her.

"What?" she said, her face all grizzled and childlike.

He wasn't aroused. His penis flopped comically to one side. He cupped it with one hand, protectively.

"I've fixed it," he said, looking like he might cry; for a moment she was moved.

"Fixed what?" she asked.

"The ants," he said.

Jesus, she thought, he had more to worry about than that.

Outside, by the pool, a line of ants trailed toward the house like ellipses.

# BAUDELAIRE'S DOG

On a table by the pool under a white umbrella a dozen strawberries sweat in a chilled glass in the sun. The dreary pockmarked young film director is raising a hand in benediction for the waiter. His companion is taking papers from his briefcase. "Justice," the director declares, "is when both sides are equally pissed off. There ain't no lightning bolts no more. You want ideas you steal them, you just piss with them enough so no one recognizes them. That's originality." He looks at his watch impatiently. "Isn't he supposed to be here by now?"

And all the while the L.A. waiters twentypercent about, their have-a-nice-days taken to the ultimate declension. You're welcome, you're very welcome, you're so very much more than welcome, hi, my name's Leslie, I'll be looking after you today—note looking after, not bringing you food but actually looking after, a mother, a father, the one sole person in this dogshaggin' town who *cares*—oh you left your hand-reared sea-salted friséed fish tartare, you didn't like it? IS EVERYTHING ALL RIGHT? And out of the shimmering mackerel pool soar a throng of blonde beauties in perfect sync singing, "We're sorrrryy, we're sooo sorrrrryyy."

Three English rock journalists in free rock T-shirts flop at the next table, looking like cigarettes with the tobacco half poked out. Slumped in total indifference, eyes darting about like guppies, they gob imaginary spitballs of cynicism at everything they see. They order one of every dumb-named cocktail on the menu and charge it to the record company while slagging off the star.

"The man's a human B-side."

"Total fucking vegetable."

"IQ of room temperature."

"With the air-conditioning on."

"Look over there, isn't that Pussy?"

As they turn to look an entourage comes out from the lobby. Record company VP, toothy blonde PR girl, a man like an aristocratic psychiatric nurse. And Cal West in a sea-blue suit. He's moving carefully, like he doesn't want to make a mess or make them mad. For all that he looks better than he has in a long time. A hand pressed into the small of his back guides him through French windows into the press conference room. The three English journalists pick up their drinks and follow. Two women in one-piece bathing suits dive into the water and rise to the surface simultaneously like water ballet stars.

The director peels off the top sheet of paper. He reads aloud, "He was in a car with his girlfriend when it happened—very pretty. Underage. 'I think I'm losing it,' he said, and he did. He started screaming, so did she, and when he finally pulled over she ran off. She hitched a ride and called the cops from the next town. When the ambulance arrived he was comatose." He looks up. "It *is* Pussy," he says to his companion. "I thought it was her." He watches her stretch languidly on the sun lounger, then sit up to sip her drink. He feels his cock ossify as he watches her suck on the straw.

Dignified and willing his clothes not to suffocate him, Cal sits at the long table on a raised platform in the press conference room. The record company VP on his left taps a microphone. The therapist on his right pats his hand. People are piling tape recorders on the table in front of him, then shuffling to the back of the room to get a drink. He is conscious of the hot blush of a shaving rash on his throat. His suit emphasizes his new leanness. Only his hands have stayed fat. His fingers are sweating; he thinks they might smell shameful. He looks at the crowd of journalists, faces he doesn't know. Some look bored, most look curious. He catches the eye of an attractive young woman at the back of the room who is smiling at him expectantly and holds her gaze. The therapist is smiling too, and whispers in his ear, "It's going to be fine, Cal. You'll survive."

They said he'd die but he didn't, though his brother did. Flapping like a fish as he held him underwater, no one would suspect him, he never left the house. A freak wave, they told him. He thought about it often, his brother on the sand like a white plumped-up pillow, the people all tanned flesh gawking, sea slapping like wet flip-flops, while he was home in bed. He dedicated this new album to him, his first solo record. The one his record company is telling all these people is his best work yet. He knows it isn't really. It would have been if that guy who looked like Buddha let him use the songs about horses, but all they ever want from him is songs about the sea.

The PR announces that anyone who has a question should stand up and give their name and the name of their publication.

"Nathan Jacobs, *Rolling Stone*. Hi, Mr. West. First, welcome back." There is a small round of applause.

He had spent the last—how many?—one-two-three-four-five years in bed. Half a decade. A twentieth of a century. He gives his head a swift little shake. His brother and sisters had carried on without him, brought in a replacement—"For now," they always said, "until you're better." They wrote some awful songs. They raked the thesaurus to find new words for "sea" and "sadness" while he lay in bed ignoring them, happy as a bug. He lived in his pajamas because they made no demands on him. Bed smelled of home. Bed was his whole existence. He came to have a dozen different words for "bed," like Eskimos have for "snow."

"My question is: What exactly was it that brought about this comeback?"

"God," Cal answered. "And Dr. Hank."

The man on his right shook his head dramatically. "No, Cal, you did it."

"Did your family have anything to do with your decision?"

When Cal had showed no signs of ever wanting to get up and write again, his family had panicked. They begged and bullied. They hung seaweed in his window. They put a clock by the bed and set it to wake him up with the sound of ocean waves.

"My family," Cal answers, "have always been behind me."

"A long way behind," the man from *Rolling Stone* mutters, and sits down.

"Hutchie Hutchins, the *Sporting Times*." The PR and

the record company VP both swing their heads round simultaneously and give him a strange look. "Your new fitness regime has become almost as famous as your music. Would you tell us a wee bit more about it?"

He spat out his vitamins; he tantrumed for junk food. They brought him ice cream by the barrel, donuts and Cheerios. But he still wouldn't write. He grew as fat and white as a spaceship. He was like a planet with stars revolving around him. He had never been so happy, and dreamed happy sea-slapped dreams.

"Dr. Hank can tell you about it," says Cal, handing him his microphone, resulting in a pained squeal of feedback.

"Hi Cal, John Davidson, freelance, here. Your parents, reportedly, have said they do not approve of your solo record and that families should stick together."

It was a year before his mother came to visit. His father would drop by once in a while, his sisters all the time, he didn't know what had happened to his brother, he just disappeared. But Mom never could deal with sickness, not even when they were kids.

Overweight, overjeweled, overblonde, looking like the decor in a Polynesian restaurant, Mom bent over him and butted his cheek with hers. She smelled of Revlon; the bed smelled of babies. Her clipped nose was wrinkled. Her voice was strained and distant like in a computer game. On and on it droned and zapped; he wasn't even listening, he'd quite forgotten she was there until he was suddenly aware that his hand was inside his pajama pants, automatically tweaking. His mother's voice grated across his balls like a saw. He sat bolt upright like a sleepwalker, and his mother started from her chair. He hadn't said a word to her—nor to anybody else all year. His first words were to the man sitting by his side at the press conference, helping him face these people who are insolently gawking, clutching their free copies of his CD under their arms.

Another one stands up—ah, it's the pretty young woman he was looking at earlier. He doesn't catch her name, her magazine sounds like it's called *Pulp.* He likes the word. He taps out a rhythm on the table as *Pulp* ping-pongs around in his head.

"I'm curious about the closing song on your new album"—he notices she has an English accent—"'The Dream of a Dying Wave.'"

It was late afternoon. He'd just woken up after late-afternoon dreams, little things with pickaxes climbing up the bedposts onto the pillows and carving some sort of message about fame on the inside of his arm, when a knock came at the door. He was startled as he woke to see the sun starting to set, as if the world were somehow inside out. The room smelled wet and cottony. His father ushered a grave man with pale blue eyes into the room. He was lean, lightly tanned, glittering in voluminous white clothes. He walked to the window and sat on the inside ledge, posed in soft focus against the pink outside light.

"It sounds like you're saying that you're the dying wave?"

The man gazed at the pale slug underneath the sheets. He pressed himself up athletically and walked toward the bed. Cal's sisters appeared at the door, one at a time, and stood against the far bedroom wall. The man in white paused, rummaged in his pocket, and took out a small pink sachet. He slowly tore it open, pulled out a small scented square. He sniffed it like a love letter, then rubbed it over his hands. He crunched and dunked it into the trash can by the bed. He put his clean fingertips together as if in prayer. He held his hands over the shape in the sheets as if holding an imaginary basketball. His father shuffled, awkward, like a little boy in church. His sisters simply stared. The man muttered, maybe hummed something, looked up at the ceiling, then bent and whispered something in his ear.

"Except of course a wave never dies."

He clears his throat to answer the Englishwoman.

A noise came from Cal's pillow. A gluey, phlegmy cough. Then a voice, once so famous, that used to sound like angels, that sounded like everything good and innocent and American that ever was, a voice rusty from disuse started to say something. His father and sisters leaned forward and strained to listen. It sounded like: "Those big strong horses sure are sweaty, aren't they? I tell you one thing, though, if they're hungry enough they'll eat anything you give 'em and that's a fact. Well, that about solves the mysteries today. I repeat, that about solved the mystery of the great field of horses, did it not." His family crept around his bed like shepherds round the cradle and sucked in the words as if the greatest fibers of thought were contained therein. Or at the very least some new lyrics. Therapy, the man in white told them, would not come easily or cheap.

And now he sits at the conference table, people are still firing questions, some spray-painted little shorthaired escapee from a Gap ad is napalming him nonstop with a flashgun. They're asking about God, his politics, his girlfriends, how he writes his lyrics and where he buys his clothes. Does he still take medicine? Does he still need treatment? Does he feel like a spokesman for the damaged of the world? What is his philosophy? What is his ambition? Is it true he'll have a psychic with him on the road? People with funny accents want a special message for the fans in some country or another on the tour.

"Jason Parker, *Picture Palace*. How is the biopic coming along. Will Leonardo DiCaprio be playing your brother? How does that make you feel?"

And at once he has a vision; it almost starts him laughing. Dawn hasn't broken, and he's on an empty beach. He's walking in the shallow water back to his bedroom, the sea tossing his brother around and around like a loose sock in a washing machine.

"Ban Johnstone, *Rag*. It's odd you should write about the sea with such innocence and romance when it killed your brother and your band?"

And he sees his therapist shake his head and hold up a hand and he hears the record company man thanking everyone for coming and sees him nod at someone at the other end of the room who puts on the new record. "A masterpiece, and I don't use the word lightly. A little more volume please?" And he sees waiters glide in and out of the badly dressed crowd with overdressed trays of canapés. Half the journalists hover like famine victims by the table where they're setting up the buffet, the others crowd the platform wielding photos to be signed or waving cheap tape recorders for a personal word or two for the four dozen listeners of a Maltese radio show. The small group of writers drinking Perrier with the PR, who'll get exclusive interviews later in the day, look around, smiling smugly at the rabble, like courtiers granted an audience with the king.

The English woman wrote in her notebook. "The record swoops and soars like a constipated seagull. Last time I looked it was still at number one. Baudelaire, I read somewhere, came back from the city one day with a bottle of rare perfume and held it out for his faithful dog to smell. The dog recoiled in disgust and started barking. Oh, wretched cur, said Baudelaire, or some such, had this been a turd I'd brought you you'd have sniffed it with delight, rolled on your back, and sought out the butthole whence it came. But I offer you something exquisite and you want to kill it. Thus you, my loyal dog, are just like my public, and I shall give you all the shit that you deserve."

The director waits for Cal outside under the cool white umbrella. He looks at his notes, his cell phone, his watch. A skinny girl with fifties tits walks deliberately close by him, jutting, pointy, bouncing pink rockets aching for employment. The director feigns indifference and stares at the pool. The sun singes a scar across the surface of the water.

# AUTOGRAPH

Spike's cock was on fire. It throbbed out a 2/4 rhythm in perfect time with the car alarm that whooped outside on the street. Where he was or what he was doing there he had no idea—his eyes wouldn't focus in the unlit room and his head was a sponge—but if the raging in his groin was anything to go by, he'd given her the going-over of her life.

The question was who?

As if in answer, a figure materialized at his left side, which his blurred vision split into two, one circling the air several feet above the other, neither of them quite identifiable. A hand tapped firmly on the inside of his elbow—same tempo as his cock and the car alarm; it was all the operative fragment of his brain could do to stop the inoperative portion from singing along with "Another One Bites the Dust" by Queen. Spike went to sit up but his arms and legs wouldn't move. He was paralyzed! No, that wasn't it, he was strapped down—he could see by double-chinning along his body—arms, waist, and legs, to a table. Naked. Before his brain could assess this information as good or bad, a needle slipped into his arm. Then another slid just as deftly into his genitals. As Spike sank back into unconsciousness, his penis shivered and uncurled, shuffled a short way down his thigh, and pumped itself up in slow motion, before stretching out on his stomach, where, like a beatnik Muppet finger, it casually beat out time.

Minerva Smallwood did not have Spike's autograph. The thought popped into her head as she was making the rounds of the geriatric ward, plumping pillows, emptying pans, folding the papery patients upright in their beds like origami birds. Actually she didn't have anything of Spike's. In all the time she knew him, she hadn't asked him for anything and, obligingly, he never gave her anything, except, one time, the clap. Luckily, Minerva, as a nurse, had easy access to drugs. She had long ago figured out that her easy access to drugs was a big reason why Spike had stuck around as long as he had. The other reason, of course, was that she kept him. She smiled to herself—just one more female patron of the arts. A couple of the old folk smiled back at her. The rest looked at her blankly with milky eyes, even when she spoke to them. She'd noticed that the elderly developed a selective sense of hearing, hearing only what they want to, carrying on, undaunted, on their own track. Just like rockstars. Just like Spike. Although, technically, she reminded herself, he wasn't a rockstar for most of the time she knew him. And he wasn't even Spike, he was Mike.

It was a matter of personal pride to her that she'd never tried to cash in on their relationship. Friends would say, "You ought to tell your story," whenever they read the latest of his young lovers' kiss-and-tells. "You could write a book, make a fortune, tell them what he's really like. 'Spike's Split Personality'—half arsehole, half cunt." She would just laugh and say it was all dead and gone, not worth digging up. As she picked shriveled carnations out of the cheap service-station bouquets that dotted the ward, she could imagine journalists coming after her when the story got out, asking her how she felt about him after all these years, did she still love him or was it hate? And she could see herself answering that she never even thought about him. Which was true—most of the time.

Quite when Spike had started making daily appearances in her masturbation fantasies, Minerva could not precisely say. But at some point, during a long stint of night shifts—thrashing about on her bed in the morning like a solo wrestler, all pointless gestures, trying to force herself to sleep and knowing it was impossible, soon cars would be revving up outside, then the pneumatic drills would start, and the highly strung Greek woman would be screaming at her kids upstairs—that's precisely what he did. A van had pulled up outside her basement window, its radio blasting Spike's new single. Suddenly the singer materialized on her bedroom ceiling. She found her fingers sliding between her thighs, and moments later she was sleeping like a child. Over time Minerva developed an entire catalogue of Spike scenarios— damned imaginative, some of them, but perfectly harmless. After all she had done for him it was the least he could do for her.

If they asked her in the interviews, she could put her hand on her heart and say the last thing she wanted or expected was to see him in the flesh. When Spike's mother died and Minerva sent his father a condolence card, it was simply because she'd liked his parents and they'd liked her. Plus she felt bad thinking that on her deathbed his mother would have seen that tart in the *News of the World*'s description of her firstborn's genitals. No, she pictured herself explaining, she was not obsessed with Spike's sex life, it was just rather hard to avoid it.

The invitation came out of the blue. "Hello, Mini?" The voice on the phone sounded so much like Spike's that, even after all this time, her stomach vaulted. "It's Jim Mattock, Mike—I mean *Spike*'s brother. How are you? Sorry to just call you like this"—they hadn't spoken in years; he sounded shy, embarrassed. "Is this a bad time to talk?"

She assured him it wasn't, that she was fine, and he said that he was okay too. She said she was sorry about his mum and asked how his dad was holding up.

"Oh, I'm sure you remember what he's like." Jim sighed. "Doesn't want to talk about it. Sometimes you're not even sure if he realizes that she's gone. But that's why I'm calling. Because one thing he did say was that it would be really nice if you could come to the funeral on Thursday."

"Me?" She heard the surprise in her voice. Jim heard it too. "Mum," he stumbled, "kept telling Dad, just before the end, how she'd wished you and Mike had got married. I think"—he laughed nervously—"she was disappointed that neither of us had managed to give her grandchildren." Jim was gay. And Spike was Spike. "I mean I can quite understand if you'd rather not?" But she found herself saying she would.

The night of the phone call, Minerva couldn't sleep. The reason she couldn't sleep was because she couldn't masturbate. Lord knows she tried, but the screen refused to show her fantasy movies of Spike. Just the real, flesh-and-blood Mike, memories she'd successfully walled up for years coming back to wind her up. When she gave up, got up, and poured the last third of a cheap bottle of white wine into a glass, her nerves were shrieking. Once again he had simply upped and gone, and she was left with nothing.

The next night was the same, and the next. The night before the funeral, Minerva lay in bed, rigid. Her jaw clenched, her temples pounded. She reached for her sleeping pills but stopped herself; they always made her look like a zombie the next day. Her fury at herself for caring how she would look for Spike made her tenser still. Her hand worked away uselessly like a worn-out sander as the memories flooded back.

She was living the other side of the river when he first moved in with her. A poky bedsit in Finsbury Park, conveniently near his parents' place. Whenever he ran out of sofas to stay on or girls to doss off, Mike would go back to the bedroom he shared with his younger brother. Not the ideal setup for a rock musician—which is how he'd introduced himself to her that night at the bar.

"Hi, I'm Mike. I'm a rock musician. Who are you?"

Her friend was more enthusiastic. "Great! What band are you in?" But it was Minerva he was looking at. He had the most symmetrical features she'd ever seen on a man, like those impossibly chisel-chinned drawings of boys in the picture stories in teenage girls' magazines. "He liked you," her friend said afterward, a touch resentfully. "He likes himself more," she replied. She started dating him the following weekend. Two weeks later a friend dropped him off with a guitar and three bin-liners of clothes.

She could see that room as clearly as if she were standing in the doorway—the sink in the corner with the broken cupboard underneath and the shelf above it with the mirror on it. The chest of drawers with a two-ring electric stove propped on top. The fireplace where they put the milk bottle to keep it cold. And most important, the bed, some indeterminate size between single and double, the sheets always smelling of damp and sex. Their sex life was adventurous and unflagging. The drugs came later—Mike's idea. Because of her work she'd never thought of them as recreational. He changed her mind.

One night she'd come home from the hospital late to find a bunch of guys she didn't know sitting on their bed, bawling along to some loud, distorted music she didn't know either that was playing on her cassette player. "Mini, my most beloved," Mike said grandly, "meet my band: Spike. What you are hearing is our first hit single." Not long after, Mike razor-cut his hair and started using the name Spike for himself. He was not a natural democrat. For the next six months all her spare time was spent ministering to the group—funding their rehearsals, watching them play in an endless series of grim London pubs. Sometimes her nursing friends would come along to plump out the crowd. After a while it didn't need plumping. Girls would hover by the back door after the set. Not that Minerva was the type to ask, but he told her they meant only one thing to him: record sales.

"I belong to you, Mini," he declared as she woke up one afternoon—she was on night shift. "Body and soul. Especially body. Now close your eyes." He was naked and holding something behind his back. She did as he said. Crouching by the top of the bed, he took one of the black nurses' stockings he was clutching and tied her wrist to the top of the headrest. Minerva opened her eyes.

"I've got to get ready for work," she protested. He went over to the other side of the bed and tied her right wrist. Then he sprung onto the bed and sat on her legs to hold them down. With a felt-tip pen he started to write "SPIKE" on her stomach. "Here!" he announced. "I'll even give you my autograph."

"Stop it, you're tickling," she said giggling. When he got to the letter I, he slid inside her. The pen fell on the bed, leaching a widening blue circle where it lay. That was the day he told her the band had been offered an American tour. Low-budget, bottom-of-the bill, but America for all that. "Brilliant." she'd said. "Give me the dates and I'll try to book some leave." "That wouldn't be cool," he answered. "Most of the time we'll be in the van or sharing the one room. Next time," he soothed her, "it will be different." It wasn't. The second tour they'd agreed that none of them could bring their girlfriends. The third was a much bigger affair, almost three months. Halfway through he agreed, albeit reluctantly, to her coming for a long weekend in L.A.

He'd given her a shopping list and she brought it all: teabags, Branston pickle, Dexadrine, and Valium in squat brown prescription jars made out in her name, and all of the British music papers. They were scattered over the motel bed when he tugged off her panties and mounted her moments after she arrived. "Am I in there?" he asked. She only worked out later he was referring to the *N.M.E.*, which he was reading over her head.

The next afternoon, out by the pool, everything felt wrong. Her legs looked deathly white in the harsh light, against the Heinz-baked-bean-can-colored sky. The air was weirdly buzzing, and hot and dry as dust. The same could be said for her vagina on the long plane ride home. Nothing, fortunately, that antibiotics couldn't cure.

Her hand automatically pulled back from between her legs. She stared grimly at nothing. Then suddenly, out of nowhere, a vision appeared, a multicolor CinemaScope special that covered the ceiling and walls. Spike. He was naked and more aroused than she'd ever seen him. His hands were tied down with stockings. She was looming over him. The orgasm knocked her out cold.

When Minerva woke up the next morning, the clouds had lifted. She cast a joyful eye on the grimy swab of South London visible through the condensation on the windowpane. When her cat pushed the door open and jumped onto the bed, Minerva picked her up and kissed her. The cat squirmed free and followed her into the kitchen, where she put a bowl on the floor and a frozen croissant in the microwave. While the water huffed through the coffee machine Minerva whistled—and she never whistled. She felt as if she had gone to sleep in midwinter and woken up on a fresh spring day.

The service was not until one o'clock, so she took her time showering and picking out what to wear. Naked in front of the full-length mirror, she sized herself up like a stranger— pretty good shape for a forty-year-old, a bit on the wiry side maybe, and overdeveloped in the calves from being on her feet all day. Her hair was still lush and long, though, and thanks to the bottle, dark brown. She pulled on a pair of opaque black tights, a black knee-length skirt, and a white cotton blouse.

"I look like a schoolgirl," she told the cat. "But Spike likes schoolgirls, doesn't he? Actually," she frowned, "I look like a hotel maid. This won't do." She scrambled out of the clothes, leaving them on the floor, where the cat instantly curled up on them and went to sleep. Rummaging in the back of the wardrobe, she emerged with a black silk skirt, form-fitting, slightly longer, and a small, tight, long-sleeved shirt. In a drawer she found a long-abandoned suspender belt and delicate black stockings. A pair of high-heeled ankle boots finished it off marvelously. Turning from side to side, Minerva felt quite triumphant.

She decided to leave early, practice walking on her high heels to the tube station, and then find a café in Finsbury Park. The station escalator was out of order as usual; the sign apologizing for the fact had curled at the edges with age. A newer sign at the bottom of the stairs had another apology, this time that the destination indicator wasn't working either. Minerva walked down the stairs, carefully, and along the platform to the one unoccupied bench. Opposite was an enormous advertising poster recruiting nurses for a private hospital. A perfect family—attractive blonde mother, little girl with pigtails, freckled young boy—was gathered around a bed where a ruggedly handsome man was lying in the kind of pajamas that a ruggedly handsome man would never wear. Hovering behind them, her expression simultaneously calm, concerned, efficient, simpering, and pathological, was a nurse. Florence Nightingale twinned with a stewardess. The caption on the ad said, "Daddy has cancer but the nurse made him feel better."

"The poor bastard's dying, for crying out loud. What did she do? Give him a blow job?" Minerva realized, when several people on the platform looked up from their papers to stare at her, that she had said it out loud. She found it almost overwhelmingly funny. Normally she would have hated this kind of dishonesty. That was the thing with Spike: When he'd phoned from the States to say their engagement was off—*phoned*; didn't have the balls to tell her to her face— he said it was because she didn't show enough interest in his "art." If he'd just told the truth, said thank you very much but he didn't need her services anymore, then fine. Before any dark thoughts could settle in on her sunny mood, the rush of cold air that heralded the train's arrival swept them away. It also blew her coat open; a couple of male passengers glanced appreciatively at her legs.

Minerva took the long route to the church, past the winos and garbage congealed around the station exit, stopping at a Turkish coffee shop and ordering an extravagant pastry. Her taste buds were as hypersensitive as the rest of her. The cake and coffee seemed almost unbearably sensuous. Everyone around her seemed to be sparkling. She had to remind herself she was going to a funeral. Avoiding the street where the Mattocks lived, she headed for St Jude's.

She was a little taken aback to see security barriers and immense men looking like concert bouncers monitoring the activities of a smallish, mostly female crowd. Some were carrying thin, cellophane-wrapped bouquets. For Spike, Minerva suspected, not for his mother. A steward with a clipboard ticked her name off the list and guided her into the churchyard. "I'd rather stay outside in the air for a few moments, if you don't mind," she told the usher who came over to take her to her seat. She leaned on the wall to one side of the Gothic doorway, watching people arrive, none of whom she recognized.

Eventually the hearse pulled up, camouflaged with flowers, and right behind it a black limousine. Jim was the first out, helping his father from his seat. Spike was the last. He looked about, as if he were checking out a new venue and wasn't entirely sure where his dressing room was. Some of the crowd were calling out his name. Spike turned to look at them. Jim waited a few moments for Spike to join them, then gave up, took his father's arm, and walked him toward the entrance. As they approached, Minerva tried to slip away, but Spike's father spotted her. Coming over, he took her warm hands in his own cold ones and said, "Thank you, dear, it was good of you to come. Will you come and sit at the front with us?"

Jim correctly interpreted her look and said, "Come on, Dad, we'd best get seated." As he passed Minerva he whispered, "Sit wherever you feel comfortable. See you afterward back at the house?" When Spike turned around to follow them in she found herself flushing scarlet. But he didn't notice her. He walked straight past her and into the church.

She couldn't help staring at him from her seat at the back as he stood at the lectern, reading a passage from the Bible. He looked even brighter in the gray stone building than he had in her home movies. His suntan looked almost tangerine. There were too-bright highlights in his hair. His suit, perfect for Los Angeles, looked too flash for a weekday afternoon in Finsbury Park. He was still a good-looking man—though nowhere near as attractive as he'd been in her fantasy last night. Still, Minerva felt herself moisten.

Suddenly she was aware that Spike had stopped reading. He had started to sing, a cappella—a song he said he had just written for his mother. When it was over he announced the title, "Love Eternal Guaranteed," as if it were a performance, and received a small, inappropriate round of applause. His father's head had dropped onto his ribs. Spike's brother had his hand around his shoulder, comforting him, awkwardly, as if even this small physical display of affection might be too much. Afterward, when the three men walked together back along the aisle, there were cameras flashing outside. She saw that a second limo had arrived. Spike gave his father a fleeting kiss on the cheek, gripped his brother's shoulder for a micromoment, then turned and got into the limo and went back to his hotel. He didn't show up later at the house.

There was something Mike always used to say to Minerva: If you want something badly enough you will get it; all you have to do is focus and it will come to you. He was absolutely right. Minerva had no real plan for what she wanted but she certainly wanted it badly enough and, once she focused on it, it was astoundingly easy how quickly it presented itself.

The morning after the funeral, at 5.45 A.M., just as Minerva was coming on duty, a young hooker showed up at the outpatient department. Drug-thin but extremely pretty and with incongruously large breasts, she gave her age as eighteen but looked years younger. Her discharge was easily dealt with. Harder to fix was a methadone habit that neither her prescription nor the duty doctor were willing to satisfy. When she left Minerva followed her and took her to one side. Surreptitiously she slipped some flunitrazepam into the astonished girl's hands.

"There's more where these came from, and better," Minerva whispered.

"What do I have to do?" said the girl, switching quickly into professional mode.

"Your name's Laura, right? I'm Minerva." She led the girl outside. The plan that Minerva now outlined to the girl came to her immediately. They agreed to meet later that day at a café in the center of town. Minerva knew that the other nurses would understand and fill in for her if she said she needed to go home early, that she was still feeling raw.

Nursing a cold cup of coffee, Minerva was getting frightened that Laura wouldn't show when the young woman strutted through the door on kitten heels, twenty minutes late. All heads in the café turned. As she had promised, she had made a real effort with her appearance. She was wearing a short, flowery skirt, and a low-cut gypsy top and was swinging a small straw bag. Minerva thought she looked about twelve. Spike would not be able to resist. Minerva had been given Spike's hotel and room number by Jim. There was a password, he said, to get past security, and she'd written it all down. She wrote it down again in the café for Laura on the back of a sealed envelope.

"I'll give you the rest when we're done," Minerva said. The girl seemed trustworthy, but it wouldn't help to tempt her to take what she had and run. Minerva had told her—convincingly, because it had been the truth—that Spike was an old boyfriend who had ditched her when he became famous and that she figured he owed her one last favor. The young girl would get into Spike's bed and get him warmed up, then slip him some Rohypnol—the date rape drug—and Minerva would come in and take over. Laura thought it a brilliant idea. The only thing she couldn't understand was why Minerva wasn't wearing something sexier. She looked like a hotel maid.

In the couple of hours since she had left the hospital, Minerva had done a few necessary errands, then changed into the sensible black skirt and white blouse she had originally planned to wear for the funeral. She had also hired a rental car, which was on a parking meter outside. They got in and she drove to Mayfair. As they approached the hotel she dialed the number on her mobile phone, gave the password. When Spike answered the phone she hung up. Minerva stopped outside the hotel on a double yellow line and got Laura to repeat her instructions one last time. Then she kissed her on the cheek, wished her luck, and watched her walk through the hotel door. A police car pulled up behind her. At the same moment a car pulled out from a parking place directly opposite. She smiled in the rearview mirror and swung straight into the space, turned off the engine, and waited. The girl didn't come out. Everything was working fine.

At the allotted time, Minerva went into the hotel. No one said a word to her; she looked like one of the maids. As arranged, Laura had left Spike's door unlocked. Minerva pushed it open gently, just an inch, and could see Spike's arse pumping up and down. Laura spotted her and brandished the small hypodermic the nurse had given her, giving her the thumbs-up. Minerva nodded and Laura rammed the needle in Spike's butt.

Minerva slipped into the room as Spike sank onto the bed. She closed the door, deftly propped him up against the headboard, and started to dress him.

"What are you doing that for if you plan to fuck him?" asked Laura.

"I'm taking him back to my place," said Minerva.

"You're joking! How do you plan on getting him out in this state?" But, like Spike said, it was all a matter of focus. Minerva poured a glass of water and dropped a pill into it. She plumped up his pillows and held the glass, professionally, to his lips. His eyes opened. He looked at her strangely, as if he might know who she was but his brain had no idea what to do with the knowledge. If she had expected a flash of wordless understanding, it never came.

He let himself be pulled off the bed, his arm draped over Laura's skinny shoulders. Together the pair tumbled past the front desk like drunks; again no one said a word. Minerva, who was focusing harder than ever, followed a few steps behind.

They managed to prop him upright in the backseat of the rental car, Laura sitting next to him and making sure he didn't fall, until Minerva dropped her off at Waterloo with money and pills. Driving carefully, avoiding speed bumps, Minerva headed south to her flat. She focused hard on avoiding red lights, on keeping her nosy upstairs neighbor from looking through the curtains when they arrived, on maneuvering Spike safely down the basement steps, through the door, and into the kitchen. When she propped him on the kitchen table, he played his part perfectly and passed straight out. Her cat came in through the flap and jumped onto Spike's stomach, lifted a back leg, and had a wash.

Minerva shooed the cat outside. She shut the door and peeled off Spike's shirt and trousers. With the stockings she wore to the funeral, she tied his wrists to the table legs. Two pairs of tights secured his legs, while a third pair, pulled apart at the crotch, were wrapped tightly around his waist and under the table. She went to the sink and washed her hands. Spike was moaning quietly to himself. She bent over and felt his forehead, then dabbed antiseptic on the inside of his elbow and squeezed in the contents of a syringe.

By the time she had fetched a bowl of water and towels, he was unconscious. Meticulously she washed his stomach, where the cat had been, and then his genitalia, gently stretching back his foreskin, lifting the scrotum carefully to clean in all the creases. She patted him dry with a clean cloth. Then she prepared another hypodermic. Prostaglandin E1, fascinating drug, was a favorite with the junior doctors. It was made to treat babies with respiratory problems, but someone had discovered that injected into the penis, it gave an enormous erection that lasted for over an hour. Almost instantly, Spike's flaccid cock unfurled and puffed itself out like a party blower.

Smiling and singing to herself, Minerva opened the small black case on the chair. It was amazing what you could get in South London with ready cash. She plugged it in—it had a nice long lead, so she didn't need an extension cord—

and placed it carefully by Spike's waist. She leant over him and lifted his penis. The tattoo gun roared into action.

It was an awkward position to work in, and the vibrating gun was harder to control than she had anticipated. She skidded as she started to make the first straight line. Shaking a little, she stopped, wrung out a clean tea towel in the bowl of water, and dabbed at the blood. His groin had an angry, swollen blush. It might be a better idea, Minerva thought, to write the letters on first with a pen. With a firm grip on his cock, she started outlining on the underside MINERVA. But it didn't look right. She rubbed the letters out with cotton wool and antiseptic and started again. This time, using capitals, she spelled out the name he had always used for her, MINI.

Blood and ink mingled as the needle pierced his skin at thirty jabs a second. Every now and then she would stop and dab on some antiseptic. When it was finished, she stepped back to admire her handiwork. Good, she thought, but somehow unfinished. There was nothing on the top side. She pulled it toward her, elongating the skin like chewing gum, to write on her last name, SMALLWOOD.

Spike drifted in and out until the pain slapped him back to consciousness. He could hear a hysterical, high-pitched buzzing that seemed to be coming from way off. There was a weird taste, like burnt peppermint, in his mouth. His cock was burning. He tried to get up, but he couldn't move. By jamming his chin into his chest he could make out an enormous, blurred stiffie. And someone holding what looked like a power drill. The look on his face was more surprised than hurt.

"Fuck me," he said, and passed out.

# PATRON SAINT OF AMPUTEES

Prostrate on a poolside lounger at the Eden West hotel, Pussy was bored. Only boredom implies an awareness of something lacking and Pussy wasn't conscious of anything. Brain-dead, only no one had bothered to switch the life-support machine off. She stared at the pool, because that was where her head was pointed, at the halfhearted whorl around the inlet pipe. Almost noon. Four hours until the meeting. Drinking was an option, but whether it was worth numbing numbness was far too complex a question. A waiter deposited a large vodka and cranberry juice on her side table. The decision appeared to have made itself.

*Lyrics.* Pussy took a sip. The middle-aged actor on the other side of the pool nodded at her glass, raised his own, and smiled. He appeared to have a baby's head stuffed down the front of his beige swimming trunks. This surprising sight momentarily unblocked her brain. Sitting bolt upright, picking up her notepad, she wrote down the first words that came into her head: "It's a scary world but we have to live in it. The wind is blowing in hot from the desert and all the scorpions have wings. There are dangers all around, animals that eat you, things that sting." She scribbled it out. She couldn't shake the dream she'd had the night of the party.

She was a little girl at the seaside, digging in the sand with a plastic spade. It was nighttime but the moon was bright. The little girl dug deeper and deeper. She peered down into the hole, and at the bottom was an enormous crab, transparent, like a giant jellyfish with claws. There was something trapped inside its body; it looked like a human head. As the moon moved over the hole like a searchlight she recognized it as her own face, as it looked on the last Pussy album sleeve. The crab crawled up onto the sand and a crowd of people came rushing over. The crab tried to dart back into the hole, but they fell on it, ripping it to pieces, stuffing it into their maws. Pussy woke up with Churchill's penis in her mouth. "Good morning," he said. "I've written you a poem."

They were on a king-size bed in Irving's guest house. A wall of windows looked out onto the ocean. Everything in the room was gleaming white. It looked like it had been re-painted every night, like Disneyland, when the crowds have gone home. She remembered the poet–TV presenter inter-viewing her on camera at the party, but she had no recollec-tion of picking him up. Quite pleased with herself that she had, though. She checked him over. Young, good body, big fleshy mouth. If you fell off a tall building and landed on those lips you would walk away unbruised. A mouth, Pussy decided, made to give, not to receive. Gratifyingly, he was a fast learner.

"FOCUS!!!" she wrote on the notepad, outlining each letter and adding three thick exclamation points. Studio time was expensive, as Jack, her manager, kept reminding her, and if she didn't like the lyrics *he'd* written then she'd better pull her fucking finger out and write her own. Jack was pissed off with her. Pissed off that she wouldn't record his songs. Pissed off that she didn't take him to Irving's party. Even more pissed off that she hadn't come back to the hotel that night and had missed the record company meeting the next morning. She rolled over and grabbed her bag, dug out her cell phone. She was about to call Churchill at the TV station when some odd sense of decorum made her stop. She rummaged in her bag for her cigarettes and then, remembering she was in California, frowned and put them back. She saw that slotted into the cellophane wrapper was the limo driver's business card. She had asked him for it after he dropped her off from the party. His private number was handwritten on the back.

Stepford Limo Man. That was her first impression of him. Immaculately dressed and primed, like an actor about to hit the boards. He had picked her up, driven her to the beach, and waited in the car for her all night—she'd had so much to drink she'd forgotten to tell him to go home. When at around noon she had stepped out into the sun, bleary, hair wet from the shower, and found him still waiting in the driveway, he'd just smiled discreetly, not a word of reproach, opened her door, got back behind the wheel, confirmed her destination, and asked if there was anything she needed before pulling smoothly out of the drive.

They'd gone a short way when she noticed for the first time the icon that hung from his rearview mirror.

"Saint Dymphna!" exclaimed Pussy.

The driver saw her lips move in the mirror and pulled back the glass divide.

"The medallion," she said. "Saint Dymphna."

"That's right," he said. He looked a little taken aback.

"She's my favorite saint," said Pussy. "So beautiful. I first heard about her when I was a little girl, and I fell in love with her. Her father tried to have sex with her and when she said no he chopped her head off. She died a virgin. No head." She gave a little laugh. "But in every other way intact."

"The patron saint of amputees, lost souls, and the mentally deranged," said the driver.

"And which of those," she asked, "are you?"

And, staring straight ahead at the road, Reeve explained how before he'd become the perfect limo driver he was the consummate Jim Morrison. He told her about the car crash, the epiphany, his Doors tribute band, the hit TV show he had in Germany, and how one day he woke up and knew he couldn't do it anymore and just walked away. Pussy listened with rapt attention. She shuddered as if someone were walking over her grave.

The limo might have been a funeral car, the way that half the people it passed on the street stopped and stared with a mix of curiosity and respect. "Heaven," said Pussy, "will have tinted windows. So I can see them but they can't see me."

"I heard somewhere," the driver answered, "that they reckon there's a separate heaven for celebrities. Because even after they're dead people still want to look at them."

"Paparazzi angels." Pussy shivered again. "An eternal audience of ghosts. That *would* be hell. You know," she said after a long silence, "when I was young I was so afraid of crowds that my mother took me to see a psychiatrist."

"Not a great career choice then." She saw his smile in the rearview mirror. She smiled too, but her face was sad. She told him everything that had happened to her—the deaths, her disappearance. The glass screen separating them made it feel like a confession box, a separate confession box for celebrities, with minibar, TV, and luxury, cream leather seats.

"Hey, do you have to be anywhere?" she asked. He shook his head. "Then would you mind if we just drove around for a while?" Reeve indicated left, turned at the lights, and headed back down to the beach.

It was late afternoon when she got back to the hotel.

Jack was in the lobby, fuming. He might have been there all night. "Where the fuck have you been? No, don't tell me. I don't fucking want to know. What I *do* want to know is, is it really worth me being out here working my fucking ass off for you"—she noticed he said "ass," not "arse"; he was already going native—"when *you* can't be arsed"—this time she noted he said "arse"; curious—"to show up for the most Crucial Fucking Meeting of this Whole Fucking Trip? Hello?" He was talking now through the mouthpiece of his headset, his voice all humility, charm. It was the record company A&R department; they'd finally taken his call. "Sure," he said. "Absolutely. I know how busy he is. But you know those stomach bugs, I thought it best if she see a doctor. Absolutely. Thursday at four? Thank you *so* much. I appreciate it, truly." His voice switched back to a bark. "You hear that?" Pussy nodded confirmation. "And you look like crap," he said, though actually he thought she looked beautiful. Bruised mouth, too-bright eyes smudged with yesterday's eyeliner, tangled brown hair. She'd ignored all his entreaties to bleach it blonde again.

She changed her mind about calling Churchill. Maybe she'd get him to write some lyrics. See how Jack would like that. Talking of Jack, he was heading in her direction, dressed in swimming shorts and clutching a towel. "Drinking?" he said, glowering at the empty glass. "I don't have to tell you how important this afternoon is."

"No you don't." She shot him a radiant smile.

"Good," he said. "Three o'clock. On the dot."

"It's only twenty minutes away."

"I'm not taking any chances this time. And don't stay in the sun too long—I want you clearheaded." He dived into the pool, swam a length underwater, stood up in the shallow end, shaking his dark hair like a Labrador, and got out. Two women in one-piece bathing suits dived in from opposite ends of the pool, surfacing at the same time, like water ballet stars.

Pussy tried to get a waiter's attention, but they were all running about fetching endless cocktails for a knot of unprepossessing young men in shabby rock T-shirts. English music journalists. She recognized the type. She followed their gaze to the lobby door, where a party of people were coming through. Pussy recognized the psychiatrist first— Dr. Hank's picture had been all over the Shining Star Institute. And then she saw Cal West. Her heart skipped momentarily; even stars get starstruck. She'd read that he was making a comeback. Right now he looked like he wanted to run away. Hank's palm, flat in his back, ushered him into a roomful of people.

At three on the dot, like he said, Pussy's room phone rang. "The car's out front," said Jack. "I'll come by your room."

"It's okay," she said. "I'll meet you in the lobby."

"Now?"

"Now."

"If you're not there in five I'm coming to get you."

Stuffing her cigarettes in her purse, she took a last look in the mirror. She'd made an effort; Jack couldn't complain. She was wearing the tiny silk dress she wore to the party. It had worked on Churchill.

"Well, look at you!" Jack held out his arms in the lobby. "Sweetheart, you're fabulous. Just the ticket. Come on, let's get this business over with and then I'll take you out on the town." There was something they needed to talk about; he couldn't keep putting it off. He guided her into the car, simultaneously announcing to the record company through his mouthpiece, "We're on our way." The car cut into the sluggish traffic and joined the slow crawl west through the tunnel of palms down Sunset Boulevard.

The A&R man kept them waiting more than half an hour—part punishment, part power game. Finally they were fetched up to the conference room. Various record company people Pussy vaguely recognized were shuffled around an enormous polished table shaped like a giant surfboard. "Well hey there!" said a plump, tanned guy with the formless face of a fetus dunked in Orangina. "Terri Allen. My favorite star." He got up from his leather seat and wrapped a soft arm around Pussy's small shoulders, pumping Jack's hand with the other, then handed them back to the assistant to lead off to the far end of the table where the lighting was harsher. "Make yourself comfortable." The room appeared to have been specifically chosen for its discomfort factor.

"I believe you know everybody?" He indicated around the table, then looked at his watch. "Okay, let's hear what we've got." All eyes followed Jack as he walked the length of the room to the sound system. The A&R man rolled back his chair, put the disk in the machine, pressed play, then put his feet up on the table.

"Well," he said, a full minute after the music had stopped. His colleagues looked at him to see what facial expression they should wear, Buddha Boy's having remained benignly neutral. "I gotta say you are one *sweet* sounding woman. Your voice is better than ever, babe. Pure fucking sex. *Better* than sex. Those young boys are gonna cream on you all over again. But"—he swung his feet back down to the floor—"a voice as good as that comes with a

price, and do you know what that is? Songs that do it justice. A *band* that does it justice.

"I love you; as far as I'm concerned you're fucking
*perfect.* If it was down to me"—he waved his girlish arms
around the room—"I'd shake this company upside down by
the ankles and give you all the money we got and say, take
it, do what you want with it, just make me a fucking record.
But the market, babe, is a bitch. It don't give a fuck that you're
a genius. It don't care that you can sing anybody in this goddamn business, anyfuckingbody you can name, under this
table. You gotta give the market what it wants, and what it
wants is you *plus.* Plus great songs. Plus great band. And
angel, I'd be hurting you if I didn't tell the truth, I don't hear
them here."

Everyone at the table shook their heads mournfully
from side to side.

"But I tell you where I *do* hear it," he said, slapping
both palms on the table, his face all joy. "*Pussy.* There was a
reason that band was a legend, and in these troubled times
that's what the people want again."

She shot her manager a desperate look, but his eyes
were glued to Buddha Boy.

"What the world needs now is *Pussy.*"

"*Pussy,*" echoed the voices around the surfboard.
They were all smiling; a couple of true disciples slapped the
table with their palms as well. "*We want Pussy!*"

"Frank," she whispered, "you've got to say something."

"It's all right." He patted her thigh, soothingly, his
focus on Buddha Boy a little impaired by the electricity that
shot through his groin as his hand touched her bare flesh.

"Then I'm saying something," she hissed. She stood up. "I'm sorry," she said, "but I thought it had been made clear. Pussy is not an option."

There was a long silence. She could hear a bass beat pulsing through from the other side of the wall. Buddha Boy pushed himself out of his chair and walked over to them, his shoes creaking on the polished floor. They weren't new; he didn't do much walking. He shooed a young man out of the chair next to Pussy's and sat down. She was sandwiched between the A&R man and her manager, the three of them close enough to sing harmonies on one microphone.

Buddha Boy took her hand in his, stroked it slowly. "Let's talk a moment," he said, gently, "just you and me. There's nobody else in the room, Terri. They don't matter. This is all about you, your music, how to make it work for *you*. That's all I'm here for, you and your music. You gotta trust me on this one, work with me. The environment has never been tougher than it is right now. People aren't buying records like they used to. They want a sure bet, something they know they're gonna like. It's a comfort thing. And they like Pussy—no, no," he said, squeezing her hand, "don't say anything, listen to me for a moment. One Pussy album. That's all I'm saying. To get your face back out there. And when it's the monster hit I guarantee you it will be, then we'll do a solo album."

She pulled her hand away, shook her head. "Pussy is dead."

"And ready to rise from the ashes," smiled Buddha Boy.

"That is not going to happen," she said, working hard to control her voice.

Buddha Boy hesitated for a moment. Jack was staring at him hard, willing him not to divert from their agreed script. But the A&R man was in improvising mode. He looked her straight in the eyes. "I've spoken to the band," he said, "and they're a hundred percent up for a reunion."

She was enraged. "I'm sorry you've wasted your time and I'm sorry you decided to talk to Robbie, Chas, and Johnnie and get their hopes up. But they know how I feel about it. There *is* no band. There never can be. When Taylor died, Pussy died."

She could feel Jack stiffen. She turned around. His face looked strange. "I'm sorry, sweetheart" was all he said.

Buddha Boy took both her hands and rolled himself forward so that his round mouth almost touched her ear.

"Taylor is up for it too."

"What did you say?" Her cheeks reddened. "That is not funny." She turned to her manager. "Let's go." Jack was sitting, rigid, in his chair. Under the bright halogen, his tan had turned a purply gray.

"Come on," she said. "We'll find another label. That is so sick."

"I'm sorry," he said again, "truly I am. I only just found out myself."

"Found out *what?*" she screamed.

"They tracked him down and flew him out. He got in yesterday."

*"What are you talking about?"*

"Taylor's alive. They're in the studio. We weren't"— he shot the A&R man a hostile look—"going to even talk about this before . . ."

The words ceased to register. Just lips moving; plaintive sounds. The room was churning. In a single moment, the thoughts and questions and images coalesced and a great clump of vomit shot from her mouth. Buddha Boy rolled his chair out of range, untouched. She puked voluminously, violently, over herself, over the giant surfboard. A couple of people looked away. Buddha Boy sat and watched her. Jack jumped up, held out his arms.

"Get the fuck away from me!"

"She's upset," he announced, ludicrously. "Look, I think it's best if you give us some time alone?"

Buddha Boy nodded, "Okay, everyone, we'll take five." Some of the people around the table seemed unable to move. "Come on!" he ordered, and strode ahead of them. As, one by one, they joined him, his secretary came over to where Pussy sat, carrying a stack of extra-large promotional T-shirts. She tossed one over the biggest pool of puke and put the rest on the chair next to Pussy. "The rest room's out of the door, second left," she said softly. "If you need anything, we'll be two rooms along," then followed everyone out.

Pussy sat up straight. Her face was scary; even her lips were white.

"Where is he?"

"In the studio, Burbank. The rest of the guys are there. We'll go over as soon as we're out of here. Or maybe you want to see him somewhere on your own first? Whatever you want, just say it. I swear to you, Terri, I didn't want this to happen." His eyes were pleading. She'd seen that face so often before on men who were desperate to fuck her.

She stood up. Her legs were shaking. Her silk dress was gummed to her with sick.

"Can I get you some water? A drink?"

Ignoring him, she peeled off her dress, folded it, and put it on the table. She was naked except for her shoes. He didn't look away. She took an oversized T-shirt from the clean pile and pulled it on. Cal West's big round face on the front of the shirt smiled quizzically up at her. The shirt almost touched her knees; Taylor's resurrection seemed to have shrunk her. "I'm going to get cleaned up," she said, picking up her bag. Jack moved to come with her. "I don't need your help." On the way to the door she passed the shelf where the woman had found the shirts. Grabbing a promo baseball cap bearing the logo "Shoot 2 Kill," Pussy walked out.

At the end of the corridor in the stairwell, she piled her sticky hair on top of her head and jammed on the baseball cap, back to front. She might have been a teenage boy. She went down the stairs, into the lobby, and past the receptionist, who didn't give her a second look. Out in the street she jaywalked the busy road to the shopping center opposite, lighting a cigarette as she walked. On a low wall at the back of the car park, she sat smoking fiercely, cigarette after cigarette, blowing out thick chutes of smoke at disapproving passersby. Reeve's card was still stuck there in the cellophane. She dialed his private line.

Five cigarettes later, the limo pulled up. Reeve jumped out and opened the back door.

"Where to?" he asked.

She'd assumed, when she called him, that she would go to Taylor. She changed her mind.

"The fuck out," she answered.

"You got it," he said, swerving around and heading for the exit. Saint Dymphna danced on her chain.